QUALITIES OF MERCY

RICHARD V. BARRY

Winterlight Books
Shelbyville, KY USA

Qualities of Mercy
by Richard V. Barry

Copyright © 2009 Richard V. Barry
ALL RIGHTS RESERVED

Second Printing—November 2010
ISBN: 978-1-60047-366-1

Printed in the U.S.A.

For Katy,

Who enriches, inspires and enlivens my life – but whose greatest gift is the joy and laughter we share –

My gratitude and love

FOREWORD

Picture a huge stone castle complete with rounded turrets and a massive front gate. It sits majestically alone on a wide, flat plain in the heartland of America, surrounded by vast acres of barren soil, with a long, curving road snaking its way up to the entrance. The walls of sandstone blocks have turned muddy brown with age and exposure to harsh weather.

Seeing this edifice from a distance, a child might fancifully imagine it to be a medieval castle with knights and soldiers and lords and ladies and courtyards and dungeons. In reality, this castle does have soldiers to guard it and lots of ladies and lots of dungeon-like cells, for it is a state-operated maximum security prison, the Ashroken Correctional Institute for Women. It was built at the end of the nineteenth century and was originally intended to house male criminals. That was long before the rampant spread of illegal drugs and surging violent crimes by women necessitated a change-over to accommodate the growing number of female prisoners.

If you take the road leading to the prison in the opposite direction, you eventually come, after a twenty-minute drive, to a small hamlet called Dixonville. Here you find one short main street containing a unisex beauty shop, a combination grocery, hardware and liquor store, a diner, a coin-operated laundry; two tiny churches (Methodist and Baptist), and a bar and pizza shop.

1

On the half-dozen side streets, you see small ranch houses and single-width trailers jumbled together on flat, irregular plots, marked by skimpy grass and low, sparse shrubs. The entire area has an unkempt, worn appearance, as though the inhabitants were too busy or too tired to care about its neglected look. Ninety percent of this hamlet's population, male and female, works at the prison, while their school-age children are bussed for over an hour to a run-down, overcrowded public school.

Continue along the road another thirty minutes in the same direction, away from the prison, and there is a dramatic change in the topography as the terrain gets hilly and green, and tall trees rise in abundance. You can even glimpse two small lakes. Off in the distance, on impressively large tracts of land, between five and fifty acres, you can spot sprawling colonial houses and even bigger modern homes. They're surrounded by lush lawns, tennis courts and swimming pools, all tucked neatly behind whimsically designed front gates anchored by stone or concrete pillars. This meticulously tended, carefully guarded spot is called Claremont Heights.

One hundred percent of the men in this opulent community are highly successful. Nearly all of the men, but only a few of the women, travel for an hour each day, each way, to the thriving Midwestern city where they practice their professions, steer their companies, sell their merchandise and earn handsome rewards.

Most of the women of Claremont Heights have the luxury of being full-time housewives and mothers who occupy their days running their households and supervising the help: year-round maids and, in the summer, gardeners and pool people. They play bridge and tennis; they golf on a private and exclusive golf course, or swim in an indoor pool at the equally exclusive country club where the exercise room is usually crowded, and personal trainers, who also make house calls, are always in demand. They host luncheons, and eagerly participate in local charity events. Their children go off to a private school on the outskirts of the city, about forty minutes from home. In short, most of the women are fit, most of the children are spoiled, and most of the men revel in vanquishing their competition and secretly delight in the symbols of their rise to wealth and high status.

Claremont Heights has a main street that runs for three blocks and boasts only upscale establishments: a gourmet country store that offers breakfast and lunch in a cozy room with a fireplace, and sells homemade jams, breads, cookies and pies; an inn that offers ten individually designed guest rooms and The Chanticleer Tavern, the only public drinking house; a bakery that offers custom-designed cakes for every occasion; two beauty salons; a nail salon; a florist; a large liquor store featuring expensive wines; a branch of Barclays Bank of England; a gourmet cheese shop; a dog grooming business; a three-story colonial-style professional building housing an architectural firm, a legal firm and assorted doctors; a ladies' accessory shop, where belts start at seventy-five dollars, and shoes and bags soar into the stratospheric range; one large, stone, Gothic-style Episcopal church and one much smaller, contemporary-style Catholic church; and a dance studio where the young girls of Claremont Heights take up ballet, tap or jazz dancing, depending on their weight and inclinations.

The road alone is the symbolic thread between the denizens of this exuberantly affluent suburb and the people of the prison: the inmates, guards and clerks. Though separated by a modest distance, to travel across that distance—in any way beyond the physical sense, in either direction—would be like going on an expedition to the moon. By choice or circumstances, few people ever make the journey. This is the story of one woman who did, and how her life was forever changed because of it.

1

A sudden, screeching sound slicing through your ears! No matter how many times she heard the clang of the main prison gate closing behind her, an involuntary shudder rippled through Emma Granby's tall, lean body. Her reaction never changed. She would quickly remind herself that she was here at the Ashroken Correctional Facility as a volunteer. She had the freedom to leave whenever she wished. Still, being cut off from the outside world, behind looming stone walls, for even a brief time made her feel claustrophobic and anxious. Then she would think of the women prisoners entering through that gate and its harsh, resounding closing signifying their loss of freedom for five, ten, twenty years or more – sometimes for life – and she would feel sad.

"Place all bags and shoes on the table!" Commanded the fat, female guard in a tired voice as she paced back and forth behind the long, metal table. All the prison guards wanted to be called "correctional officers," but neither the inmates nor the volunteers referred to them by that title.

Emma and the three women who had passed through the prison gate with her moved toward the table to deposit their belongings.

The inspection procedure for all visitors was thorough, even for those volunteers like Emma who had been coming to the prison twice a week on Tuesday and Thursday afternoons for nearly two years to prepare inmates to get a high school equivalency diploma. Emma had learned never to carry her pocketbook but to leave it in her car. She slipped off her shoes and presented them along with her book bag for inspection. The guard ran her hand around the inside of Emma's shoes—a known place for hiding contraband—and inspected the bag, moving its contents around, but never looking at Emma. The guard muttered "Okay" and Emma slipped into her shoes, picked up the bag and moved quickly toward the far end of the barren, gray-walled chamber where another female guard, black, rail-thin, with a perpetual frown, was waiting to wave a metal detector wand around the contours of Emma's body. While she recognized the necessity of this scrutiny, she also resented it, feeling diminished and untrustworthy.

"Move quickly, ladies!" shouted another guard who had just entered through a locked door at the end of the room.

Emma had learned to automatically obey all voices of authority at the prison, and walked quickly toward the third guard, offering a shy smile but getting neither smile nor eye contact in return. Most of the guards remained as rigidly indifferent and removed from the volunteers as they were from the inmates, and their cold, impersonal attitudes were as much of a psychological hurdle for Emma as this passing-through process to reach her destination. She relinquished all power at the front gate: her identity; her freedom; the usual courtesies she was accustomed to from her position in the outside world. Today she buoyed her spirits during this ordeal by focusing on the anticipated joy of seeing her good friend Mercy. But thinking of this kind soul instantly brought an involuntary frown to Emma's face, for something was clearly wrong with Mercy.

2

As she hurried down the long corridor that led to the administrative wing, Emma couldn't help but reflect on the long and circuitous path that had led her to this volunteer prison work just two years ago. Married to a successful architect and the mother of three children, by that time all in school, Emma, at thirty-six, had suddenly felt restless and vaguely dissatisfied with the life that, she knew, many people would have envied. She, however, who had been raised as an only child and encouraged by her parents, two casually indulgent professors, to be reflective and self-centered, now found herself, in some vague, unfocused state, searching for more.

She lived with her husband and children in an old colonial house listed on the National Register. Her clever husband, Oliver, had modernized and made comfortable the interior without violating its character. Her children, Jonathan, twelve, Jeremy, ten, and Susie, eight, were happy, well-adjusted, unusually even-tempered kids who, surprisingly, at this early stage of their lives, exhibited a self-possession and self-sufficiency that reflected their mother's personality. They required little of her, and she occasionally reproached herself for her lack of spontaneous intimacy with them.

How like me they are when I was their ages, she often thought. Her own parents, while intellectually engaged with

Emma, were emotionally distant. As far back as she could remember, these two brilliant, somewhat diffuse individuals had treated her like a third adult in the family, and she had gradually retreated into herself, becoming her own person at a precociously young age. Now, as a mother, Emma felt herself repeating the pattern of her parents'. She loved her children and was dedicated to their care and welfare, but she found it difficult to relate to their emotional needs. When she thought about this situation more precisely, she admitted that she found it difficult to perceive and decode their emotional needs.

With the success of Oliver's busy architectural practice, most of Emma's household duties had been delegated to Marta, a cheerful Latino lady who cleaned, laundered and cooked five days a week. This household assistance left Emma with little to do between the time when she drove her kids to the end of the long driveway of their ten-acre estate, where the bus picked them up, and then greeted them at the same spot in the afternoon. On the weekends the family often ate at the local country club where Oliver made important contacts for future clients and Emma, on automatic pilot, played the role of the perky, witty and dutiful spouse.

From a half-hearted sense of duty, Emma was active in the Parent Teacher Association of her children's private school and regularly attended all their recitals—band for Jonathan, ballet for Susie, chorus for Jeremy—and all their sports events. She never had to remind them to do their homework and only occasionally was she called upon for help. She drove them to equally large, well-cared-for houses for play-dates and chatted breezily with other overeducated, stay-at-home mothers, all of whom were masters of small talk about nothing in particular.

At that point in her life Emma had become acutely conscious of, and quietly resented, the defining titles that applied to her: soccer mom, upscale suburban housewife, country club matron. Their membership in the exclusive golf club was, both Emma and Oliver insisted, strictly for business aims, but she harbored the secret feeling that he enjoyed mixing with the local titans much more than she did.

Seeing forty approaching over the horizon, Emma felt an urgent impulse to break out of the narrow mold that had come to delimit her life and in which she saw no change for many years. Yes, she thought with a reflective candor that had always been part of her nature, I'm yet another middle-class housewife, feeling suffocated by my well-ordered, pampered life. She longed for— not romance, for she was loved and not totally ignored by her husband of thirteen years—but, rather, some new, expansive experience that would take her out of her ordinary, settled existence and give her a fresh challenge or larger perspective. Unlike her namesake, Emma Bovary, a character much written about by her English-professor mother but whom Emma found pitiful, she didn't want to run away; she just wanted to expand. As her vague longings took root and became more insistent, she knew she had to take some action.

3

"Why don't you try a new hobby?" suggested Carol Mumford, Emma's neighbor and only close friend to whom she confided her personal feelings.

As a child Emma never had a lot of friends, having been too early absorbed into her parents' adult world, but she usually had one intimate friend. This pattern continued in her adult life, and while she had any number of casual friends, Carol, two years older than Emma, was the woman she trusted to guard her confidences.

A tall, lushly attractive redhead, Carol was an anomaly in their community's conservative social set. A genuine West Coast heiress—she had inherited a sizeable estate from her maternal grandmother and still more when her much-married but childless aunt died—Carol was an immodest, unrepentant liberal who unhesitatingly expressed her frank, sometimes shocking opinions on any subject and didn't seem to care what anyone thought of her. That's the assurance that comes with lots of money, Emma had often thought.

Carol had married a considerably older man, whom she had met on a cross country train ride because, as she said, he seemed safe and secure. Gardner Mumford, an investment banker, was the polar opposite of his wife: quiet and non-descript, your average middle-age male with a slight paunch and a receding hairline. He was pleasant but quiet; she was exuberant. He was a stalwart Republican; she was a vociferous Democrat who liked to shock their friends with her ultra-liberal views. He looked and acted more like her father but, she often joked, he managed her money as if it were his own. Although they had no children, they seemed to fulfill the old adage of opposites attracting, and, in Emma's observations, they had a contented, if not exciting, marriage.

Carol's striking appearance, outsized personality and independent wealth put most women in awe of her, but she and Emma had bonded from the day Carol arrived at her door to introduce herself as her new neighbor. Having both come from pampered backgrounds, Emma and Carol discerned a rebel streak in each other that exerted a strong gravitational pull. Now they were sitting on the terrace of Carol's rambling, three-story colonial house, enjoying a late morning coffee on a warm day in early June

"I'm not the hobby type," Emma confessed in response to Carol's suggestion "I don't like sports except for skiing and I'm not into sewing or quilting or gardening, as so many women around here seem to be, and hunting for antiques or raising champion dogs has no appeal for me. I don't play bridge, can't join the choral society because I can't sing a note, and I don't even enjoy shopping that much."

Emma paused, gave Carol an apologetic half-smile and continued. "Except for reading and looking after my husband and kids, who demand very little, I'm a pretty boring person."

"You've got latent talents you just haven't explored yet. And besides, you give great dinner parties," Carol protested.

"Yes," Emma agreed, now with a full smile, "but that's about it."

Emma shook her head and the light flickered off her curly ash-blond hair, haloing her small, even features and soft brown eyes. "Remember when I tried working as a real estate agent three years ago after Susie started kindergarten? I hated it!"

"Yeah," Carol said with a wide, animated smile, displaying large, white teeth. "You lasted about three months until you discovered that bitch from the other agency was stealing your For Sale signs."

"I couldn't get into the cutthroat groove because I really didn't need the money. Besides, Oliver wasn't too happy about having a working wife. It didn't sit well with his old-fashioned ideas about being the breadwinner, or something like that," Emma said.

"There's always volunteer work," Carol suggested, pouring herself another cup of coffee. Emma gazed out across the wide lawn into the heavily treed woods that separated Carol and Gardner's extensive estate from her and Oliver's acreage.

"I volunteer at the school and I organized the church fair last year, but I'd like to try something different...something challenging...something" Emma's voice trailed off and now both women stared off across the lawn, the pool and the tennis court in Carol's back yard, giving scant notice to the two Latino workmen clipping the hedges. Finally Carol spoke.

"June Sperry—you don't know her—she's a friend of my mother's who volunteers at the women's prison. She says it's a hard scene although she likes it. But it's not for everyone."

"The women's prison," Emma repeated, trying to conjure up some image of herself in such a strange setting.

"My mother says that some of the women's stories June tells her are heartbreaking."

"I imagine they could be," Emma said offhandedly, but her imagination was beginning to stir and deep within her she felt a spark of curious excitement. Then she was surprised to hear herself saying, "That might be interesting, I think I'd like to try it," as she surrendered to a sudden impulse that was now gripping her. This might be just the kind of unusual challenge to get me out of the doldrums, she thought. So different from anything I've ever experienced. Yes, this could be exciting! And if I don't like it, I can always leave.

"I'd like to talk to June. What's her number?" was all Emma said in a casual tone, and then Carol suggested they go for a swim in her heated pool as the landscape crew finished their work and silently left the yard.

4

That afternoon Emma called June Sperry and listened to a cascading monologue, delivered with bubbling enthusiasm, in which June stated that while this work wasn't for everyone, she found it to be most fulfilling—and challenging—and exciting—and frustrating—and meaningful...and did I say fulfilling? Emma was beginning to wonder if June was a paid shill for the prison but, still, she was encouraged by June's ebullient endorsements. When June stopped to take a breath, Emma said, "I'm not quite sure where I might fit in."

"Don't worry about that," June assured her, and then asked, "What's your background?"

"I was a Greek and Latin major, with a minor in art history, in college. Nothing practical, I'm afraid."

"Do you have kids?"

"Yes, I have three, all of school age. Why?"

"Well, we have inmates who enter the prison pregnant and they're allowed to keep their babies for the first eighteen months," June explained, "so we have a good number of volunteers who work in the nursery area."

Despite her love for her own children, Emma was not particularly fond of babies and was about to express diplomatically her disinclination for this assignment, when June, still in her overexcited tone, said, "We also have a G.E.D. Program."

"What's that?" Emma asked.

"Preparing the women to earn a high school equivalency diploma: General Education Diploma," June said.

This sounded like a reasonable challenge to Emma who had thought briefly about becoming a teacher before she was married. She had even started a Master's program in education when Oliver, her steady college boyfriend, had proposed, Quickly losing her tepid interest in teaching and, she admitted, as an act of rebellion against her parents who took it for granted that she would get advanced degrees, she accepted.

Before Emma could respond, June rushed on. "I work under the prison's librarian, and spend a lot of my time in the prison's medical unit, where I bring books to the patients and read to those who are blind or can't read."

Being around a lot of sick people was not an area that Emma found appealing.

As June Sperry talked on, in her breathy, cheerleader voice, Emma tried to think of some old movie star that June reminded her of. Then she had it. Why, of course—June Allyson. How fitting!

"Why don't you call Virginia Ryan, the Supervisor of Volunteers? I'll give you her number," June said, and paused for only a second and was full-throttle again.

Emma jotted down the number that June had repeated three times, as if she were speaking to a retarded child, Emma thought, annoyed.

"I'll call her," Emma said.

"The best time to reach her is mid-afternoon. She's always looking for new volunteers. Do call her."

June's exuberance was beginning to tire Emma, whose excitement level was always mid-range, so she wanted to end the conversation quickly but June raced on, saying she looked forward to meeting Emma and if she could be of any further help, not to hesitate to call her. Emma felt like she was back in college, being recruited for a sorority—one aspect of college life she had zealously avoided. Expressing thanks, she was relieved to end the call.

5

After that phone conversation with June, Emma had moved forward in the next few days with a mixture of excitement and trepidation, frequently reminding herself that this was an experiment and she could stop whenever she wanted. She had called the Supervisor of Volunteers and arranged for a meeting the following day.

A tall, thin, good-looking woman who seemed to give scant attention to her appearance and whom Emma judged to be in her mid-forties, with prematurely white hair, Virginia Ryan was friendly but not familiar, direct but not overbearing, and thoroughly professional. Her rapid speech and crisp mannerisms suggested a woman on some urgent mission who did not have enough time to accomplish all her goals. Emma liked her. The interview lasted no more than a half-hour and it was decided that Emma would supervise a G.E.D. class with ten students.

Virginia Ryan explained that there was a series of workbooks in reading, math, verbal expression, civics and science, and a set curriculum. Inmates worked at their own pace and proficiency level and were given a review test when they completed each section of a workbook. Emma's job would be to help any inmate understand the material better if she had failed a review test.

"I'll save the pep talk and the warnings for the superintendent because he does it so well." Virginia—never Ginny, Emma imagined—said with a half-smile and a slightly mordant tone. "Every volunteer has to be fingerprinted and get a thorough background check, which takes a few weeks. You don't have any relatives or friends in this prison, I'm assuming."

"No," Emma responded. "I don't know anyone. A friend referred me to June Sperry."

Virginia chuckled. "Oh, yes, June. Quite a character! An ardent volunteer and one of our greatest boosters."

Emma smiled. As their eyes met, a ripple of understanding spread between the two women, a thin layer of shared, unstated perspective offering the first hint of a bond.

"Let's get the fingerprinting done," Virginia said quickly and Emma followed her out of the cramped but neat office, encouraged to find this competent, no-nonsense women in charge of all the volunteer programs. She sensed that Virginia Ryan could be a bedrock of support and practical suggestions as Emma established her footing in this new and strange world.

6

Emma had said nothing to her family about her possible volunteer work until nearly a month after her interview with Virginia Ryan, when she received a call from Virginia.

"You passed all the hurdles," Virginia said, "and if you're still interested, the superintendent is giving an orientation next Wednesday at 10 AM to three new volunteers. Can you make it?"

Although Emma had expected nothing less than this call of acceptance, it had taken so long that when it finally came, she responded with unexpected elation, as if she had just been offered a much-sought-after job.

"Yes, 10 AM will be fine. Thank you," Emma said after a slight pause to glance down at her appointment book that she left by the phone for quick reference. The page for next Wednesday was blank.

"Good. I'll see you then. The guard at the front gate will have your name and will direct you to the superintendent's office." There was a short pause and then Virginia said, "Thank you, Emma." These last words were said in such a sincere tone that Emma felt an instant connection with this impressive woman. Always attuned to good manners, Emma started to say that she was looking forward to the orientation, but Virginia had clicked off, and Emma smiled, appreciating Virginia's urgent sense of time.

7

That evening, after dinner, when the children had retreated to their separate rooms and Oliver and she were putting away the dishes from the dishwasher—Marta having departed after preparing the dinner—Emma spoke. She mentioned casually that the suggestion for possibly volunteering at the women's prison had been made by Carol. Oliver always kept Carol at arm's length and Emma was never sure if he approved of their friendship. She made a quick, sly study of his face for any indication of his response, but found only a blank, steady gaze. She continued with how she had followed up on Carol's suggestion and had been interviewed by the Supervisor of Volunteers and been accepted as a volunteer.

"It's only two afternoons a week," Emma explained, putting the silverware in a drawer while Oliver continued lining glasses up on a cabinet shelf on the opposite wall of their spacious kitchen. "From two to four," she added quickly, omitting the fifty-minute drive each way. "Tuesdays and Thursdays. The only thing it conflicts with is Susie's ballet class on Thursdays and Marta has agreed to drive her."

She finished sorting the silverware and turned to her husband. He, too, had turned to face her, and his handsome face was set in a definite frown.

"Emma," he said, and she noted the formal address instead of Em, hon, or honey, "do you think this is wise?"

She was thrown off balance by the word *wise* and immediately resented it, as if she were some silly kid who needed fatherly direction. Before she could respond, he continued.

"I mean, that's a maximum security prison and there must be a lot of dangerous women there. Aren't you putting yourself at risk needlessly?"

In her excitement she hadn't thought of that, but now that her husband had mentioned the risk factor, it only added to her sense of adventure. She smiled. "No, Oliver, there's hardly any risk at all. I would only be meeting with ten women and there's a guard present at all times. My risk factor is far greater driving to the prison than entering it."

The frown lines and deeply worried look had not left Oliver's face. "I can understand why you might wish to get out of the house and find something to challenge you, but why, of all the things you could possibly do, would you choose this?"

Emma returned his intense gaze with a slight smile.

"It's because I do want a challenge, as you put it, and nothing else really appeals to me. I've never been much of a joiner, as you know, and anything that involves social clubs or meetings of bored housewives, no matter how worthy the cause, is not for me."

"Are you bored?" he asked with a hint of little-boy hurt edging his voice. "With me? With the kids?"

She quickly covered the distance between them and, taking his arm, laid her head against his shoulder. "Of course not, darling," she said, patting his chest. "But you have your work that you love, besides me and the children, and I would like to try this. It's only an experiment and I can leave at any time."

His arm tightened around her shoulder as he drew her closer to him and spoke softly. "Okay, Em, if that's what you really want, but, remember, it will be an experiment for all of us."

He kissed her gently on her forehead and nuzzled her hair. She rested contentedly in his arms, happy that she could begin her new adventure with her husband's blessing. The door was opening—or more accurately, the prison gate—and she would walk through it, not knowing what she might find on the other side.

8

On Wednesday Emma had attended the orientation for new volunteers—in this instance, three other women and herself—in the superintendent's office. The superintendent, a tall, burly black man with a huge neck and hands the size of baseball mitts, had a gruff manner that matched his appearance. His twenty-minute orientation consisted mostly of prohibitions. Don't share personal information about yourself! Don't wear jewelry! Don't bring money or any valuables into the prison. Don't form any special bonds! Don't do any favors for the inmates!

Emma listened attentively and for the first time began to glimpse the world she was about to enter. Her thoughts began to stray. Maybe Oliver was right. Maybe this isn't the wisest thing to do. She began to feel uneasy as challenging questions flitted across her brain, and her palms grew moist. Then she reminded herself what she had emphasized to Oliver: This was only an experiment and she could leave whenever she wished. Calmer now, she returned her attention to the superintendent who was concluding the orientation.

"Always remember that the inmates have been found guilty by a jury of their peers, but some of them are extraordinarily manipulative and see you as bleeding hearts ready to be seduced. Each of them has a hard-luck story that could make you weep, but keep your distance, be wary at all times, and don't do anything they ask you to do for them without checking with Virginia. Thank you for volunteering and good luck."

Virginia Ryan, who had been sitting at the side of the superintendent, saw a startled expression settling over Emma's face. She seemed deep in thought. Up to now, Emma's obscure fancies about working in a prison centered mostly on herself. She had pictured herself helping women master the basics, serving as a tutor, really, to women eager to improve their lives. She also secretly relished the shock value of announcing to other people in her social circle that she was working in a prison.

With almost gleeful anticipation Emma could picture the surprised, puzzled, uncomfortable expressions of the wives at the country club, adjusting their diamond tennis bracelets and muttering banalities. Isn't that nice! How interesting! How fascinating! Now the superintendent's words had caused her to shift her perspective to the inmates and to speculate about their personalities, their lives, and their possible view of her. This shift aroused an endless stream of questions and doubts and even fearfulness.

As Emma rose from her seat to shake hands with the superintendent, she felt a new level of disquiet, and was relieved to see Virginia Ryan smiling at her as she approached.

"Emma, follow me to my office and I'll give you a set of workbooks and review tests that you can look over before your first class next Tuesday," Virginia said in her typically crisp manner that somehow reassured Emma. But throughout the weekend, as she reviewed the workbooks and thought about her introductory remarks to her students, her family noticed that she was noticeably edgy and distracted. What began as an adventure in her mind was now looming ahead of her as a fearsome challenge. When Tuesday arrived, she was filled with nervous apprehension as she drove to the prison, parked her car and approached the prison gate.

PART TWO

9

Hurrying along that long corridor to the administration building where she taught her class, Emma's thoughts flitted between the past and the present. In the nearly two years that she had been following this route every Tuesday and Thursday afternoon, except for holidays and family vacations and the week she had had the flu, so much had changed.

She arrived at the end of the corridor and simultaneously rang a bell and held up her official ID badge against the small window in the door. The guard on the other side of the door buzzed her through, nodded but did not return Emma's smile. After all this time, I don't know why I bother, Emma thought, but she knew she would continue to acknowledge a human connection with the guards and try to break through their indifference. Just now, however, she had more important things on her mind.

Mercy, Emma's classroom aide, who had been with her since Emma's first class, was coming back from the medical unit today, and Emma would see her after a two-week absence. How much she had missed her!

Emma smiled at the thought of that toffee-colored face with the smooth Jamaican skin belying her fifty-three years, the huge, expressive dark eyes and the wide mouth always ready to smile, displaying dazzling white teeth. She could never have gotten through the last two years without Mercy's help and gentle guidance.

It was Mercy who, greeting Emma at the classroom door and sensing her nervousness on her first day, had calmed her by saying, "The ladies are very nervous about meetin' their new teacher. The last one was here only two months but she had no patience and hollered a lot. She was like a drill sergeant. You're young and pretty,"—the first glimpse of that incandescent smile—"and they'll like you."

Emma had not expected to have an aide—Virginia had not mentioned it—but as the weeks passed, and then the months, and Emma grew more relaxed and settled in, enjoying her students and discovering her capacities as a teacher, she fully recognized that it was Mercy who, through ways innumerable and subtle, guided her path and bolstered her confidence. Mercy served as a buffer when any of the students got discouraged over a poor review test score. Mercy revived Emma's spirits when individual student progress was slow. Mercy had been an aide to the previous three teachers and knew the personalities of the current ten students—five African-American, three Latino, two white—and privately and gently minimized Emma's frustration by suggestions, offered in a casual, low-keyed tone, on how best to approach each student. And it was Mercy who warned Emma when a student was trying to "get over you," which, Emma learned, meant that the student was trying to manipulate Emma for some secret purpose.

Emma, who had always been an excellent student with only moderate effort, and whose pampered life had passed seamlessly from doting, if distracted, parents to an indulgent husband, untouched by life's harsher realities, gradually learned great respect for her students whose experiences had been so different from hers. Fostered principally by Mercy, a strong group identity began to form that bound Emma and her students together in ways that she could never have anticipated, and she recognized that Mercy was the catalyst for a significant change in her life.

Under Mercy's gentle guidance, Emma quickly came to appreciate that the degree of learning in her classroom was heavily influenced by outside events to which the group instantly responded. When one of them was suffering from bad news from home—a husband or boyfriend who had been sent to prison, a grandmother who was ailing and could no longer take care of the two grandchildren left in her care when their mother went to prison, a teenage daughter who was hooked on drugs, a teenage son who had dropped out of school and was running with "the hood"—waves of concern swept across the room and no one could concentrate on workbooks. They wanted to talk.

With Mercy's quiet coaxing, Emma learned to dismiss her notions of productivity and let her students vent. Silent signals from Mercy conveyed when it was time to return to work. But it was during these group discussion sessions that Emma learned of the hardships and challenges that these women faced, both in the past and the present, as well as the underlying tensions suffusing their everyday prison life. They were caged with over a thousand women, many of whom were violent, quick to insult, frustrated and mentally unstable.

Emma realized that her ten students had started life with none of her advantages. Yet, despite all the hard knocks that life had dealt them, they still had hope for the future, as shown by their participating in this class and wanting to better themselves, even if their first parole date was years away, which was the case with several of them. They dream of a better future, Emma thought with amazement, no matter how far distant or illusory.

10

While the Verbal Expression portion of the G.E.D. curriculum focused on grammar, spelling, punctuation and vocabulary, it relied mostly on memory and workbook exercises. A few months into Emma's first year of teaching, Mercy had approached her after the class was over and the guard had escorted the women away from the classroom. They were both collecting and arranging workbooks when Mercy began to speak in her soft, lilting voice.

"Kisha wants to write to her daughter. She's in high school now and doin' fine. Would you mind lookin' over her letter and helpin' her make it correct?" A huge smile.

"Of course not," Emma quickly answered, and Mercy unobtrusively slipped Kisha's letter to Emma at the end of the next class.

At home that night, when all the members of her family had drifted off to separate sanctuaries throughout the house, Emma sat in the den reading Kisha's letter. There were many mistakes but Emma was transfixed with the content.

Dear Kianna,

I be very prode of you at High Schol – I never got
to High Schol becus I had you but you be a reel
Blessing so I don't regret nothing. I hope you know
how much I LOVE YOU so dont make my mistaks
STAY IN SCHOL – lisen to Antie Mavis—have a

desent life. I be very very prode to seen you graduat.

BE GOOD—I look for you next month – your loving
mother Kisha

Emma was deeply moved as she finished the letter and
thought of her own daughter and all the advantages she and Oliver
were giving Susie. But this mother loved her daughter just as
much and wanted the same good things for her.

Not wishing to embarrass Kisha with too many corrections,
Emma changed some verbs and corrected several misspellings but
left Kisha's private view on capitalizations and sentence structure
untouched. She also made a note to buy paperback dictionaries for
all her students since she knew already that the prison budget
would not cover such an extravagance. She immediately thought
of Inez, her teenage Latino student, who had already complained
that if you didn't know how to spell a word, how were you going
to find it in the dictionary?

Emma had given a lesson the following class on the trial and
error search, which didn't go over very well because the women
found it too frustrating

After that class, Mercy had said, "Don't worry. They'll get it.
It just takes more time. Would you like to make it into a game or a
contest? They would love that."

A few weeks later, Emma divided her ten students into five
teams of two and outlined a contest that would run for five
periods—one period each month—with points accruing for each
team who first came up with the proper spelling of a word Emma
said to them. Mercy had been right: they loved it! The
competition provided all the motivation they needed and they
couldn't wait for the next round. Emma was delighted to see that a

team would work together to find the spelling of a word even when it wasn't the day for the contest.

"There has to be some small prize for the winning team," Mercy had advised Emma. "It doesn't have to be much—just some recognition of their winning." On her next visit to the city, Emma had visited a trophy store and found a small, inexpensive gold-colored plastic trophy on which she had "Spelling Champions" inscribed. She showed it to the class and they were wildly enthusiastic, redoubling their efforts for their team to win.

The team that eventually won the trophy included Inez, who had complained about how hard it was to find the correct spelling of words. Her team partner, Lucy, a small, black woman in her forties who was mostly silent and unsmiling during class, now beamed from ear to ear and giggled unrestrainedly when, at Mercy's suggestion, Emma staged a brief, formal presentation ceremony awarding the trophy to the winners.

The remaining eight students quickly forgot their disappointment or frustration over not winning and clapped, hollered and whistled for the triumphant team. After the clamor subsided, several students shouted for the beginning of another contest, which led to a chorus of boasts about winning the next time. Emma glanced at Mercy who shook her head enthusiastically, and so a classroom tradition was born.

11

Kisha had told her classmates how Emma had helped her with her letter, and then several women had sought Emma's assistance. Beneath all the surface-feature mistakes, Emma saw the raw emotions and intense longings of these women, fighting to stay connected to their loved ones and to the world they had known outside the prison walls.

"Would you consider givin' the class some chance to write?" Mercy had asked Emma and she, knowing Mercy's oblique style in suggesting something for the class, saw at once the benefit of this in her students' academic and personal development.

Emma loved to write and from the time she was a small child, encouraged by her mother, had kept a diary. Throughout her life, she had found that whenever she was grappling with some personal problem or difficult decision, it usually helped to write it down and in doing so, she often saw the issue more clearly or from a different angle and could find a solution or make a decision. The workbooks were an artificial means of learning to write, she concluded, and could not take the place of actually writing.

Emma approached Virginia Ryan about adding a real writing component to the curriculum.

"Why not?" was Virginia's quick response. "It's a basic skill that could help them when they get out, and most of them certainly have enough time left in here, so there's room for a GED diploma and a basic writing course. Go for it! What would you need in the way of supplies?

"Just some composition books, some legal-size writing pads and an extra supply of pencils," Emma replied, and then added, "I guess we can't get around the prohibition against ball point pens."

"No," Virginia said. "Too much danger of their being turned into weapons. We've had a number of stabbings with pens that were smuggled into the prison over the years."

Emma understood.

"By the way," Virginia said, "don't think we're not grateful for all the volunteers we can get, but we do keep tabs on their performance, and in the four months since you took over the class, attendance has never been higher. The women really respond to you. Congratulations"

Emma was immensely pleased to hear this praise, not only because she admired Virginia and, she now realized, wanted her approval, but also because during these months she had struggled with herself, her doubts and concerns about the job she was doing, her effectiveness, her approach to the individual women in her class. Now, Virginia's statement erased all the previous anxiety and infused Emma with confidence.

"Mercy has been such a help," she said. "I don't think I could have done it without her."

Virginia smiled and shook her head. "Yes, Mercy is a special person." She hesitated before adding, "A good woman! But one moment in her life – one bad decision – and now she's spending twenty years behind bars."

Emma suddenly realized that in the four months that she had been working with Mercy and had been so grateful for all her guidance and assistance, she knew nothing about Mercy's background. Mercy had never offered any information about herself and Emma thought it impolite to ask. She had responded warmly to Mercy's soft-spoken, gentle ways, her blazing smiles, her encouragement and positive personality, and any notion of some criminal past had been forgotten. Now Emma's curiosity was aroused.

"What was her crime?" Emma asked.

"Murder," Virginia said flatly. "She killed her daughter's boyfriend."

Emma sat motionless in the chair in front of Virginia's desk, stunned by this revelation. She could find no clear way of reconciling Mercy's sweet, gentle nature with the cold-blooded act of murder. She had formed such a high opinion of Mercy, disregarding the fact that her aide was serving at least several years for some serious crime. Clearly there must be another side to Mercy's personality that I never see, she thought.

Through her fog of confusion, Emma heard Virginia's voice. "I'm familiar with her case. She admitted immediately that she killed the guy because he was selling drugs and trying to get her daughter hooked. So the next time he shows up at their apartment, she stabs him...multiple times."

Emma tried to avoid picturing this scene but she couldn't. Stabbing someone was so much more intimately violent and gory than shooting someone from a distance. One squeeze of the trigger and it was over, while to plunge a knife repeatedly into another person's body called for intense, prolonged fury. The sheer brutality and horror of it was making her sick. She could never have pictured Mercy performing such a heinous act, even in defense of her daughter, and she realized how poorly prepared she was to deal with women whose makeup included such potential for ugly, raw aggression.

Virginia's voice again broke through Emma's disturbing thoughts. "Never been in trouble before that, and has been a model prisoner from the day she arrived. She's had a year of college and she had worked as an aide in an elementary school, so working in the GED program was a natural fit for her."

"Yes, I can see that," was all Emma could muster, still dazed from everything she was hearing.

Virginia leaned back in her chair and the pale sun coming through the window silhouetted her face in profile. "We have a lot of women here, Emma, who are hardened criminals, with long rap sheets. But we also have a good number of inmates who were never in trouble with the law until they committed one crime—and that one crime usually involved a husband or boyfriend or other family member and some form of abuse—and they'll probably never commit another crime again. Still, they not only pay the penalty of a prison sentence but they are scarred for life. They're forever known as criminals."

Virginia's voice grew softer, as though she were thinking aloud. "Picture some moment in your life when you were at your worst—some action that you have always been thoroughly ashamed of. And suppose that this one action was made known to the world and was the only action that defined you in other people's eyes for your entire life. That's what these women are saddled with."

Virginia suddenly bolted forward in her chair and started to move things on her desk as though she were embarrassed at expressing her thoughts. "I'll see what I can do about a little extra money for the writing supplies," she said quickly.

Emma left the prison and drove home in a bleak and fragile state of mind.

12

In the following months Mercy never revealed to Emma anything but a cheerful, warm and encouraging nature, and the vivid images that clouded Emma's thoughts for days after Virginia's revelations soon receded in the glow of Mercy's smile, the soft expression in her eyes and the enthusiasm of her support.

Emma recognized that Mercy was liked and respected by the women in her class, who knew that Mercy had been a teacher's aide, thereby conferring significant status on her. Mercy clearly had a good rapport with the individual students and could quietly calm an agitated student and encourage a group sense of pride.

Emma started the practice of arriving at her classroom a half-hour early to correct review tests while Mercy arranged the workbooks and recorded test marks. In the course of casual conversations between the two women, Emma found herself sharing thoughts with Mercy—always a receptive audience—about her daily life, her children, and her husband. In turn, Mercy spoke for the first time about her family.

Her husband, like Mercy an immigrant from Jamaica, while walking home from his job as a janitor, was caught on the street in a shootout between two rival gangs and killed by a stray bullet, leaving Mercy a widow with two small children, five and seven. Before immigrating to the United States, Mercy had finished a high school business program. Now she had to raise her two children alone while working as an office temp, and she still managed to attend a junior college at night.

"I could only afford to take one course each semester because I had to pay a baby sitter," Mercy confided with a smile, "and I was a long way from my goal of becomin' a teacher, but when the girls got older I could at least be a teacher's aide. It was a lot less money but I took a second job with an accountant as his clerk-typist."

Mercy talked enthusiastically about her work as a teacher's aide, about working with a Mrs. Bellafiore in her fourth grade classroom and what an exciting teacher "Mrs. Bell" was and how much she had learned from observing the interactions between this teacher and her students. She also spoke about raising her two daughters, Hope and Charity—names picked because of New Testament references—and while she confided to Emma that Hope was having some trouble getting her life together and was currently in a California drug rehabilitation program, Charity was well settled, having married a police officer and been blessed with three healthy children.

When Emma asked Mercy if she had a picture of her grandchildren, a sad, wounded expression clouded Mercy's face.

"I don't have any pictures," Mercy said in a remorseful whisper that instantly captured Emma's sympathy. "My daughter isn't speakin' to me."

"How long have you been estranged—I mean separated?" Emma couldn't help asking.

"Since I came here—more than six years ago," Mercy said hollowly. "I get news once in a while from Hope but she and Charity are on the outs most of the time, so it's not too often."

Emma could see Mercy's visible struggle to contain her emotions so she changed the subject back to class work. Yet Emma was aware that slowly but certainly she was disregarding the one horrendous fact in Mercy's history—about which Mercy never spoke—and was succumbing to this woman's inherent dignity, gentle nature and warm personality. In violation of a prime prohibition in the prison, stressed to all volunteers, Emma was ineluctably drawing closer to her aide and feeling a strong bond.

13

The students had eagerly responded to the new writing component as a rare opportunity to open up about themselves and share their histories and feelings, since Emma, hoping to capture the interest of her class, had stressed that they could write about anything they liked. She fully expected them to write about their lives and experiences but she didn't expect such brutal honesty and openness. The more they wrote, the deeper the insights they revealed about themselves.

Emma concluded that although her students had little formal education, their thought processes showed them to be of average to above-average intelligence and one student, a young Latino woman named Mariela, gave all indications of being gifted. They had scant knowledge of the formal rules of writing and their grammar, spelling and sentence structure ranged from sub-literate to barely literate, but their thoughts were powerful and they had keen insights about the world they inhabited.

Mercy had asked Emma, "Do you think they might like to read their writings to the class?" Emma knew by now that this was a gently made suggestion rather than a question, but the advantage she saw in it was that everyone would be concentrating on the content and then she could privately correct the surface features: grammar, spelling, etc.

Emma stressed that sharing what a person wrote with the class was an option and two students, Lucy, the shy, middle-aged black woman who had won the spelling trophy, and Anita, a young Latino with sparkling eyes and a wicked sense of humor, opted to share their writing only with Emma.

The writing of these two students began to take on a strange tone of intimacy that confused Emma. They said how much they liked the class and looked forward to seeing Emma and how pretty she was. They asked her questions about her personal life, and Emma remembered the superintendent's injunction, "Don't share personal information about yourself!" They usually ended with alarmingly intimate statements: "I dream about you; I think about you all the time; I send you a big hug and a kiss."

Emma finally felt compelled to share these writings with Mercy for her guidance.

"They're falling in love with you," Mercy said with a wide grin. "Happens all the time in here. It's not supposed to, but it does. Be careful!"

Emma didn't catch the full significance of what Mercy was saying until she received a message from Virginia that one of her students, Kisha, the inmate who had written to her daughter to stay in school, had been removed from her class by order of the superintendent and transferred to another section of the prison. Kisha had been an eager student and a class leader, and Emma was mystified by her removal and went to Virginia for an explanation.

"Kisha was caught in a stairwell having sex with Lorice, another student in your class, and we had to separate them," Virginia said matter-of-factly.

Emma quickly summoned a mental picture of Lorice, a quiet, stout African-American woman in her forties who always sat next to Kisha. Emma recalled one time when Kisha was reading to the class her story about her daughter, Kianna, and how proud of her she was and how much she missed her.

Emma and Mercy always arranged the chairs in a circle for writing-sharing time—another suggestion by Mercy in the form of a question, "Do you think the students would feel more comfortable if they sat in a circle when they shared their writing?"—and, as always, Lorice was sitting by Kisha's side. As Kisha finished reading her writing, tears streamed down her cheeks and she threw herself into Lorice's arms. The class was silent as Lorice held her and patted her back, saying "There, there, honey, I know. I know," as Kisha continued to sob into Lorice's shoulder.

At the time Emma had thought it a most suitable gesture of consolation, and she waited for Kisha to take her seat before calling on another student to read. Now, with Virginia's explanation for Kisha's absence, Emma was again confronted with another aspect of prison life that she could never have imagined.

As if she were reading Emma's thoughts, Virginia said. "This is a fact of life in prison. They're doing hard time and they crave emotional attachments, and they find another woman and they become close friends and this turns to love and then to sexual intimacy. On the outside most of them would never consider a lesbian relationship—they love men—but in here it's a way to connect with another person and satisfy a basic need."

This explanation, delivered in Virginia's typically crisp, unemotional voice, was disconcerting news to Emma whose limited knowledge of sex didn't encompass such aberrant behavior.

Virginia continued. "Of course we do have instances where a male guard succumbs to the come-on charms of an inmate and they have a sexual fling. When it comes to light, the guard is dismissed immediately." She smiled and then added, "In one case it turned out to be true love, because the inmate had a baby and when she was released two years later, we heard that she married the dismissed guard, the father of her child."

Virginia reached for the phone on her desk, indicating that this was all the time she could spare Emma, but, as a final note, said, "Don't fool yourself: this place is a seething hotbed of sexual tension looking for any outlet," and Emma left her office in a reflective state with her new awareness of prison realities.

14

Emma learned further lessons from her students' writings and classroom discussions. Most of their problems and the resulting crimes, for which they were convicted, centered on men: men who had abused them; men who had forced them into prostitution; men who implicated them in drug trafficking; men who had hooked them on drugs; men who had betrayed them and abandoned them when the long arm of the law encircled them.

Mercy cautioned Emma, "I'm not sayin' their husbands or boyfriends weren't low-lifes, but they have to take some responsibility too."

Yet, as their writings suggested, they were frequently victimized by absent fathers, sexually abusive uncles and older brothers, and even crack- addicted mothers. In the case of a few women, they were the second or third generation to see the inside of a prison.

With startling clarity, Emma understood that her students had led lives so different from anything she ever experienced. Their world was where drugs and incest and AIDS and violence and homelessness and teenage pregnancy and crime and premature deaths and abject poverty were everyday experiences that they accepted and freely discussed as part of their history. Emma couldn't conceive how anyone could survive under such horrific conditions, and she freely admitted to herself that she couldn't.

Emma's respect for these women's fortitude and grit grew with each story they shared. While her life had been spent worrying about redecorating her bedroom, what dress to wear to the prom, SAT scores, college blind dates, getting a new hair style, her wedding reception, dinner parties and proper diets for her children, these women were being pummeled relentlessly with everything hard and dirty and defeating that life could throw at them. She felt self-conscious and ashamed. It was as if from birth they had been cursed with every possible disadvantage but found the will to keep struggling. No matter how many setbacks and kicks and betrayals they endured, they never lost hope for a better life. Their stories touched her deeply.

Six of the nine remaining students had children. Lorice, who had been found in the stairwell with Kisha but had remained in the class, had the most: five. Others had at least two or three children, currently in foster care or living with grandmothers or aunts.

Whenever the children were brought to see them, some coming from considerable distances, the women wrote of their happy anticipation of the forthcoming visit and then wrote of their joy in seeing them, how good they looked, how much they'd grown, how they always said "I love you, Mama," and "When are you coming home?" Tears would be shed in the retelling of these scenes by both the speaker and the listeners, and Emma, comparing the hard lives and poor starts for all these children to her own children's pronounced advantages, couldn't help but feel both pity and indignation for them.

It seemed only natural that as the women shared their histories with the class, and the atmosphere grew warmly intimate, they would ask Emma, some shyly, some boldly, about her family. Disregarding the warning about sharing personal information,

Emma felt, in fairness, that she had to share some general facts of her personal life in response to all the intimate details the women had shared about their lives. So she told them about her three children, echoing some of their phrases about being so proud of her kids. They asked her about her husband, where she had met him, what he looked like, did she love him and what did he do for a living. When she answered that he was an architect and they had met in college, they seemed very impressed.

Emma recognized that when she imparted these few basic facts about her life, her students reacted as though they were listening to a fairy tale. Just as she had learned of their lives with a sense of wonderment for all the horrifying details, so, too, did the women in her class listen to her sketchy biography with clear amazement at a life so remarkably different from their experiences. Yet the reaction of the women seemed to be one of joyful appreciation of their teacher's good fortune in having such a good life. Emma knew that she was not abiding by the prison rules for volunteers, but she couldn't be aloof or indifferent to these women who had suffered so much and, by their very presence in her class, were trying to better their lives.

When one of the two white women in her class, Helen, who wore a perpetually sullen look and was the least communicative of all the students, asked Emma in a clearly provocative tone, "What town do you live in?" Mercy, who was standing in the back of the room, silently signaled NO to Emma, causing an alarm to go off in Emma's head, and she equivocated.

"It's a small town a good distance from here, and we'll be moving soon," Emma replied in a firm voice and a direct stare, indicating to all that no follow-up question would be allowed. There was a moment of total, awkward silence, as everyone seemed to recognize that despite the friendly atmosphere of this class, the students were prisoners and Emma was not, and a huge gulf divided them. The silence was broken only when the guard tapped on the door and Emma glanced at her watch and announced that the class had ended. "Time to go. See you next Tuesday," she said cheerfully, hoping to regain a lighter mood, but, for the moment, it was hopeless, and the students silently filed out.

"That was the right answer," Mercy assured her as she gathered up the workbooks

15

"Now that the ladies feel comfortable about writin' and sharin', do you think we should move on to other topics?" Mercy asked with a big smile. Reacting to this polite nudge, Emma realized that her class was beginning to wallow in a psychodrama of past personal failures and it was time for a change.

At the next period devoted to writing, she distributed composition books with the marbled covers—many of the students excitedly recognized them from their own brief school years—and suggested that they might like to keep a journal in which they could record their daily routines and experiences.

"Not just facts," Emma urged in her best cheerleader voice, "but your feelings and reactions to things you see or hear or do."

Emma could tell from the student's chatty reaction that they liked this new writing assignment.

"Will we still share what we wrote?" asked Lucy, who had gone from being a shy, silent observer to an eager class participant, ever since winning the spelling trophy. Lucy's apparent crush on Emma seemed to have abated.

"Well," Emma said slowly, her mind only one step ahead of her words, "you can decide what you might like to share and if there are things you'd rather not share, you don't have to."

Several women were nodding, seemingly pleased with this guideline, while others were busily writing their names in their new writing books.

"Will you read our journals?" Mariela, the most gifted student in Emma's opinion, asked as a follow-up question.

"No," Emma said, shaking her head and smiling. "Journals are intended to be private conversations with yourself, and, as I said, you can choose to read whatever you want to share with the class, but you don't have to.

"Then how will you be able to correct our mistakes and teach us how to be better writers?" the determined and ambitious Mariela asked, turning down her mouth in a disapproving frown.

Emma paused for a moment before answering, as an outline quickly formed in her mind. "Every now and then—maybe once a month—I'll ask you to copy some passage from your journal that you don't mind sharing with me and, using your best handwriting and checking your spelling, hand it in and I'll correct it and return it. Is that okay?"

Most of the students expressed agreement and even Mariela was no longer frowning.

"Can we start now?" Lorice, the mother of five, asked eagerly, and several voices murmured their approval of her suggestion.

Emma paused again for only a second. "Yes, you can start by writing about our class, if you like.

"Can we describe you?" asked Helen, with a challenging undertone which Emma ignored. "Sure you can," Emma said with a forced smile. "And you can write about your classmates and what we do here and how you feel about the class. And you can be as honest as you wish and no one gets to read it without your permission."

"Good!" Helen said with a slight sneer on her lips. She was one student Emma could not fathom and Mercy, always the diplomat and the bridge builder, could offer little advice about her except to say "She's a loner and has a big chip on her shoulder. Stay clear of that one."

Holding up her own journal for the class to see, Emma said, "I've brought my journal, which I've been keeping since I was a little girl. While you write in yours, I'll write in mine."

"Will you share yours with us?" again from Helen and this time the sarcastic tone was unmistakable. Emma remained calm and responded in a neutral voice. "I have the same privileges as you do, and if I want to share some thoughts from my journal, I will."

A ripple of uneasiness was floating across the classroom as the other students recognized how Helen was baiting Emma.

"That's fair," Lucy said and several other voices said "Yeah."

Emma felt grateful for this show of support.

"I don't think I'll share too much of my thoughts—they're too hot!" exclaimed Anita, a very pretty Latino woman in her thirties who always managed to make her prison uniform look too tight and sexy. The class laughed and the momentary tension was broken. Seeing that she had no support from the rest of the students, Helen slumped down in her chair and stared down at her journal. Emma couldn't help but feel a moment of triumph and, looking to the back of the room, saw Mercy sending her a huge smile.

16

The journals proved to be a big hit with the students. In the
next period devoted to writing—Emma had established every
fourth class as a writing period, with Virginia Ryan's approval ("If
that's what motivates them, use it," Virginia had said)—they
seemed eager to share and get feedback.

A few women merely recorded their daily routines: when they
got up, what they had for breakfast, lunch and dinner, their work
assignments and what they watched on television in the assembly
room at night. A majority of the women, however, offered fuller
explorations, amplifying how they felt about things: hating having
to get up so early, hating the food, hating having to wear the bright
orange uniforms, hating their work assignments, hating some of
their fellow inmates. The women listened to each other read a
litany of hateful things about everyday prison life and they laughed
and exclaimed their agreement.

"You tell it, girl!"

"That's it, baby!"

"Yeah, Yeah."

"Damn straight!"

"You go, hon!"

Two students, Mariela and Lorice, went beyond all the others.
Lorice wrote about her aching loneliness in being separated from
Kisha, when she was removed from the class and sent to another

section in the prison. Lorice was unselfconscious in reading to the class about all the things she missed: braiding Kisha's corn rows, working side by side in the laundry area—even Kisha's job had been changed—and giving Kisha, who had a sweet tooth, all her desserts.

Emma, feeling vaguely embarrassed by Lorice's openness about her feelings for another woman, saw that in the prison culture these relationships were taken for granted, and all the other students seemed to understand and support Lorice's love for Kisha. After all, Emma reminded herself, Lorice is the mother of five children. When Lorice finished reading, tears in her eyes, she was comforted by the two women sitting on either side of her.

Mariela announced to the class that she wanted to share a poem she had written when she had gotten into a fight with another prisoner who had stolen something from her and Mariela had spent two weeks in "the box," which was the inmates' slang term for solitary confinement. These small concrete cells, deep in the bowels of this ancient fortress, had no windows.

Believing Mariela to be the one student who might be gifted, Emma was not surprised to learn that Mariela wrote poetry. The other women seemed to know this fact and an enthusiastic chorus of "Yeah, let's hear it," swept across the room. Mariela cleared her voice and read.

I CANNOT SEE THE STARS
I cannot see the stars
  But I know they are still there,
Glimmering in the night sky,
Countless diamonds in God's hands,
Showering so many gifts on all of us

I look up at night, long and sleepless
At the concrete heaven of my cell
And imagine all the stars
Brightening this world and others,
Hovering majestically above me.
I cannot really see them
But my spirit can, and does;
And I thank the Lord Creator
And ask in a humble way,
To keep me from despair,
And help me through this coming day.

Mariela finished, closed her journal and tucked her head down. Silence in the room, then a burst of applause and a chorus of praise. Emma was impressed by the emotional depth of this simple yet evocative poem. Suddenly there was another silence as Mariela and all the students in the circle of chairs turned their eyes to Emma, seeking their teacher's opinion.

"That was beautiful, Mariela," Emma said. "You really are a poet. I was truly moved." Another burst of applause circled the room, and Mariela blushed and tucked her chin further into her body.

"She's got lots more," Lucy offered.

"I'd love to see them," Emma said, smiling. "Would you share some with me?"

"Yeah," Mariela said, raising her head, looking at Emma and breaking out in a wide grin. "Mercy put a number of them in a little booklet she made. She even made a nice drawing for the cover. She can show it to you."

Emma speculated that Mercy wanted her to discover Marcela's talent without Mercy's prompting, which is exactly what happened. Emma's glance turned to Mercy in the back of the room, who was looking very pleased, but just then the guard tapped on the door and class time was up. Emma could easily tell from the smiles and lively chatter of the women as they exited the room that the journals were a great success. She also knew that she was becoming increasingly emotionally invested in her students and especially in her aide.

17

"How long to do you plan on continuing with your volunteer work?" Oliver had asked casually over Sunday morning coffee, after Emma had started her second year at the prison. She had been idly skimming the morning paper and she looked up to see an expression on her husband's face that belied the casualness of his tone. The kids were already out of the house, having taken Happy and Ringo, their two golden retrievers, for a long walk along the wooded trails surrounding the lake just a short distance from their house. Surprised by both his question and her immediate defensive reaction, Emma said "Why?"

"Because it's affecting our lives," he responded with a vehemence that startled her.

"How, Oliver?"

"In just about every way possible," he said, and she could see the reddish tinge of anger spreading across his face.

"Please explain," she said, meeting his stare while defiantly raising one eyebrow. She sensed that they were heading into unsheltered regions and mentally braced herself for what might be coming.

Oliver took a final sip of his coffee and set his mug down on the glass breakfast table with a sharp bang that almost made her jump.

"Emma, you're being consumed by this prison work. All you ever talk about anymore is your class and your students and the unbelievably hard lives they've had and what they're writing about and what each one of them said in class and how impressed you are with Virginia Ryan and how wonderful Mercy is and what a great help Mercy is and how you feel so sorry for Mercy, and Mercy this and Mercy that! It's your main topic of conversation at the dinner table, at the parties we attend and even when we're lying in bed at night and you're planning your next class in your mind which, I have to admit, isn't exactly a turn-on for me."

Emma stared blankly at her husband, unprepared for such a broad indictment including his reference to their recent change in pattern of lovemaking. Her mind was racing as she formulated her defense.

"Don't you talk about your architectural projects? Isn't that the main topic of *your* conversation? The Peterson house, for example. How many times have I heard that Mrs. Peterson keeps changing her mind and adding rooms even as the house is being built? Or your frustration with the new contractor on the Clement house. Why is your work more important than mine, even if I'm only a volunteer?"

"That's not the point," he said, clearly annoyed. "Sure I talk about my work. You always wanted me to share my work with you. It's what I do for most of my working hours and it's what's brought us a very good living standard. But your volunteering at the prison was only supposed to be a sideline, a small segment of your life—only four hours total a week, you said, but now it's expanded to much more time. You leave home earlier to prepare for your classes, you say, but then you started coming home with all those writing samples and you start pouring over them right after dinner. This has taken on a whole new dimension that is taking you away from me and the kids."

"The kids?" Emma said automatically, struggling to keep up with the barrage of accusations.

"Yes, the kids! The other night at dinner it was clear to me, and it should have been clear to you, too, that Susie was upset about something, but you dominated the dinner conversation, raving about the woman in your class who writes poetry. And Susie sat there, staring straight ahead, looking glum and dejected. But you never picked up on that, as you usually would, and every time I tried to steer the attention to Susie, you just went on and on about the poet."

Emma's mind flashed back to that dinner and she acknowledged to herself that she had been unaware of any problem with Susie. She immediately felt guilty for this lack of maternal responsiveness. The problem, she told herself, was that her kids were so remarkably self-contained and self-sufficient that they seldom needed her intercession or seldom sought her guidance. They were all so much like her when she was a child, and while Oliver was constantly alert to any hint of a problem, she respected their independence and gave them their space.

Then a question flickered across Emma's mind: Were they really like that or were they conforming to her expectations of them? Was she a caring but cold mother, as she sometimes suspected? She thought back to her childhood with her brilliant parents, ardently immersed in their academic lives, their teaching and research and writing and their intense social lives within their academic circle. When they weren't in the classroom or attending faculty meetings, they were mostly behind closed doors, each in a separate room designated as a study, to which she was, by unstated but understood rule, forbidden to interrupt them while they worked.

Her childhood home—filled with graduate students invited for tea and lively discussions or with other academics arguing about literature, her mother's field, or philosophy, her father's, or politics or religion—was a center for brilliant conversation and acerbic wit. As the spoiled child of the proud hosts, she was allowed to sit in on these sparkling events and, at a precocious young age, was indulgently invited to voice her opinion.

With sudden clarity, Emma realized that for all the theatrical displays of interest and the intermittent attention they showered on her, mostly in public, her parents, by their very nature, were not inclined—or perhaps even capable—of immersing themselves in the world of a child, so they quickly encouraged her to enter their adult world. Perhaps her early profile as a precociously mature, independent, self-contained—and self-centered?—child stemmed not from her basic nature but from her adaptation to her parents' expectations. And was she now repeating this pattern with her own children?

These thoughts confused and bothered Emma, but her focus was again on Oliver as he continued speaking.

"You seem to care more about the women in your class than you do about your own family!" was his final accusation stated in solemn tones, his eyes staring down at the table like a hurt little boy. In a flashing insight, Emma saw her strong, conquer-the-world, manly husband reduced to a pouting child, feeling unloved and insecure because he was now sharing her attention with these women and didn't like the competition.

"Oh, Oliver, that isn't true!" she cried as she reached across the table and grabbed his hands. "I'm sorry that you see it that way."

Oliver looked up but said nothing.

"Please try to understand, dear," she continued, "that this was a great challenge for me and I believe I've succeeded in meeting it and the class is going so well that I'm naturally pleased with it. Perhaps I am dwelling too much on it at home with you and the kids, but I find so many remarkable and contradictory things about my students that I want to share with you that I guess I've gone overboard. But, Oliver, it's like blinders have been lifted from my eyes and I'm seeing how people have to struggle for so many fundamental things, like love and stability and a home, that I always took for granted. These women have made mistakes— egregious mistakes—but prompted more from adverse, despairing circumstances than from cold-hearted malice, and they're paying a huge price, but they continue to hope for a better future even though the odds are heavily stacked against them."

She realized she was making a speech and stopped. Smiling and squeezing Oliver's hands, she said, "Nothing is more important to me than you and our children."

Still with a grave look he asked, "Then will you stop this volunteer work?"

She released her grip on his hands and hugged herself. She could feel the breath leaving her body in one, long stream of air, and she wondered if she had the strength to draw more air in. She saw his question as a thinly disguised ultimatum and felt trapped, defeated. She meant what she said about her family being the most important part of her life, but why did that have to be the only thing in her life? Her days had taken on a much broader dimension in meeting the challenges of her prison work, and the abilities she discovered within herself in working with her class gave her greater confidence and, yes, a satisfaction she had not felt before.

She saw her life up to this point as having been a self-contained one, indifferent to political causes and social movements and the general happenings in the greater world. She had mostly drifted through life, passively doing everything that was expected of her. The only time she had demonstrated any independence was in expressing a desire to go away to college, principally because she did not wish to be known to her professors as the daughter of their two illustrious colleagues, with attendant expectations. But this goal was quickly squelched and she easily bowed to her parents' wishes.

In college, she had enjoyed a few casual friends but stayed mostly to herself, happily immersed in books and languages and music and private musings. Then, in her junior year, a handsome young man with cerulean eyes and a warm, dimpled smile struck up a conversation with her as she was leaving the library and walked her back to her house, talking all the way. He fascinated her. It wasn't just his tall, rugged physique that ignited sparks in her imagination but his clear zest for life, his idealism and his confidence about the future that swept her out of a passive complacency, into his electric orbit. He had a fire in the belly, as she had heard her father describe ambitious junior faculty members. He asked for a date and, without hesitation, she agreed.

Two months later they were lovers, and their relationship blossomed by long distance during her senior year when he had already graduated and gone off to Princeton on a full scholarship to study architecture. She knew she loved him and that he had been her only real boyfriend, but without the daily stimulation of his company she slipped back into a passive state, starting her graduate program to become a teacher not from any strong desire but more as a pragmatic path of progress. She was happy to forgo pursuing a career when he proposed marriage.

As a self-made man, rising from poverty and a broken home, who fought tenaciously to succeed in the world, Oliver, like Emma, was an aberration, a relic from a previous era, who had escaped the women's empowerment movement and was pleased to have his wife play the homemaker, a symbolic reflection of his affluence and success. For years now she had contentedly fulfilled the role of wife and mother, giving scant thought to the small focus and insularity of her life, until unexpected stirrings came from within that impulsively led her to her prison work.

Her students, and especially Mercy, had not only opened new vistas for her but had evoked a wellspring of empathy and greater understanding They had taught her to care about others, not just those intimately connected with her. Yes, she admitted that she was deeply involved with them and wanted them to succeed in their goal of obtaining a high school diploma. This was not only a worthy goal for them but a validation of her efforts and newly discovered abilities. She couldn't leave them; it would be abandoning her own principles and giving up part of herself, part of what she was becoming.

She saw her life shrinking back to the cocktail and dinner parties, the charity balls and luncheons, with endless superficial chatter among rich, smug people whose consciousness didn't extend beyond the golf course, their investment portfolios, the business deal, the latest gossip, kids, houses, dogs and horses and, occasionally, servant problems. Their political interests focused mainly on maintaining the status quo or reducing taxes. They supported foreign wars because they were usually good for business, but she saw that none of their children were participants. Now she felt that if her life were reduced to this small world again, she would be losing her soul.

Oliver repeated his question: "Will you give up your volunteer work?"

She knew a significant moment in her life was now at hand.

18

With an intently earnest expression, Emma looked directly into her husband's eyes. She reached for his hands again and held them.

"I love you, Oliver, but I can't give up what has come to be another important aspect of my life: my ability to function productively outside the home and to be of some help to such needy people." She squeezed his hands again and smiled. "I can promise you that I won't bore you with talk about my students, and I'll try to be more attentive to the children's moods, if that's what you want, although that's always been primarily your role, and you're so good at it. But I can't stop doing this work that I consider important and gratifying. When I first went to the prison, everyone told me that volunteering in that setting wasn't for everyone and most people couldn't do it. Virginia Ryan once described it as being almost like having a special vocation. Well, I've discovered that I do enjoy the challenges and, Oliver, I've also discovered that I'm good at it. I'm a good teacher. And for everything I teach them; they teach me more."

Oliver withdrew his hands from hers, rose from the table and spoke in an aggrieved tone. "Then the children and I are no longer enough for you."

Instantly, Emma's conciliatory mood switched to one of indignant anger, and she rose from the table, too.

"That's an unfair accusation and you know it!" she found herself shouting. "Have the children and I ever been enough for you? You don't leave this house dejected day after day because you're leaving your family. Yes, I know you have to make a living to support us but don't deny that you love...that you've always loved what you do. You happily kiss all of us goodbye and go off to your office, excited about the projects you're designing and the praise that's heaped on you by your clients and other architects. You're damn good at what you do and the world gives you feedback every day and validates your worth and boosts your ego. And then you return home to enjoy your own hearth and family. And, of course, you'd say we're the most important people in your life, but that's not saying that your work isn't another very important and pleasurable aspect of your life, too."

Emma paused as Oliver turned away from her and headed for the kitchen door. Now she was speaking to his back.

"I've never been jealous of your work, Oliver—your other life outside our home—because I recognize that it completes you and makes you a fuller person, without taking anything away from me or our children. Please let me be a fuller person, too."

She watched him reach for his windbreaker hanging on a wall peg by the back door and without pausing to put it on, he was out the door and gone. Automatically, she moved to the sink with the breakfast dishes and began rinsing them before placing them in the dishwasher, still lost in thought.

Throughout their fourteen years of married life, they'd had their typical spats and disagreements, almost all forgotten now, but this one, she sensed, went much deeper, threatening a bond between them that had always been solidly secure. While she couldn't fully understand all the strong responses he had aroused by his authoritative ultimatum, she felt that he had attacked some inner, inviolate core of her being, which she had to fiercely defend or forever be diminished in her own eyes. And his.

She didn't know what to expect when he returned but she knew she would be resolute. She also knew that Oliver's way of dealing with disagreements was to remove himself from the scene and reflect on their opposing positions. He could be extremely logical in cutting through his emotions and was capable of compromise and capitulation. Still, this disagreement seemed to center on a major fault line that could result in irreparable damage, and Emma was deeply concerned.

An hour later, the kids had returned with the dogs and were in the family room playing video games. Emma was upstairs in her bedroom, getting ready for church when Oliver returned. She heard the front door open and close and then she heard his voice.

"Where's your mother?"

She couldn't discern any tone connected with the question, but she heard Susie say, "Upstairs." Her body tensed and her breathing quickened. She was sitting at her dressing table applying her makeup when he entered the bedroom and she paused, watching his approach through her mirror, fearful of what might come. Then he reached out and placed his hands on her shoulders and with a small smile said, "Okay, Em, I think I understand. But, please, a little less talk about the poet and Mercy and all the hard-knocks stories."

He started rubbing her shoulders with his strong hands and she felt waves of tension rushing from her body. His good angel had guided him and the grave danger was passed. Relieved, she put her eyebrow pencil down and placed her hands over his, smiling up at him through the mirror.

"I do solemnly promise," she said with mock formality, patting his hands. He bent down and kissed her on the neck. She patted the side of his head. "Hurry up and take a shower or we'll be late for church." she said, relieved and grateful. She finished dressing in a happy mood. She would have a lot to reflect on and be thankful for at this Sunday service.

19

Emma did make a whole-hearted effort not to talk about her prison work at home. She also tried to be more attentive to her children's moods. As she observed them more closely, she found that her two boys, Jonathan and Jeremy, despite their sixteen month-age difference, had an unusually close bond and were their own mutual support team and a closed circle of two. Good students and keen athletes, they were sunny and dependable, seldom affording their parents any concern except for typical childhood ailments. Both Emma and Oliver anticipated that the boy's friendship would be challenged when Jonathan entered puberty, leaving Jeremy behind, but, as yet, that had not happened.

Susie was definitely Daddy's girl, gravitating to her father for affection and consolation when problems arose. Emma supposed that other mother-daughter relationships might be different, although she acknowledged that her own childhood reflected a similar closeness with her father while still loving her mother. But neither her mother nor she, now as a mother, had been inclined to *girlie* things like shopping or fussing over hair or nails together.

Susie was very bright, perhaps the brightest of her three smart children; she did very well in school and was precociously mature for her nearly nine years. She loved her brothers and seldom had disagreements with them. She had a wide circle of friends among whom she was clearly a leader. She loved ballet but she also loved sports although she could never be classified as a tomboy. Her natural agility and grace in her physical coordination was evident in her dance recitals.

Like Emma, Susie loved to read and could spend hours alone in her room, reading. She was a serious child who gave an all-out effort to everything she pursued, and was always happily occupied with something. Still, Emma reflected, she's a child and clearly does have challenges and disappointments and conflicts that I'm not very attuned to, but Oliver is.

One afternoon when the boys were out of the house, Susie came down from her room where she had been reading and entered the kitchen for a soda. Emma was preparing dinner since Marta was home with the flu.

"What are you reading?" Emma asked, nodding toward the book in Susie's hand.

"*The Lion, The Witch And The Wardrobe,*" Susie replied casually."

"Oh, *The Tales of Narnia.* I loved that when I was a girl but I was older than you when I read it."

"Yeah, they're great!" Susie replied enthusiastically, clutching the soda can and her book in her hands and heading back to her room.

"Susie, can I ask you a question?" Emma said, surprising herself.

Susie stopped and turned.

"Sure, Mom," she said breezily.

"Do you think I'm a good mother?" she found herself asking with her characteristic directness, even with a young child.

Susie looked momentarily confused and Emma rushed on.

"I mean, do you feel that I'm there for you…that I'm receptive to listening to any problems you may be facing…that I'm genuinely interested in you as a person?"

Her words were tumbling out as she tried to adjust her question for a nine-year-old but she felt she wasn't making much sense. She stopped talking and gave Susie a weak, embarrassed smile.

Susie stood in the same spot where she had turned. Her face seemed to register a lengthy thought process as she obviously was not expecting such weighty questions. Then, suddenly, as if finally arriving at a conclusion, she smiled broadly and said, "Sure, Mom," before turning and heading for her room.

In plunging headlong into such a serious topic, Emma didn't know what to expect from Susie, but she found her daughter's casual, brief response frustrating.

"No, wait, please, Susie," she pleaded, causing Susie to obediently stop and turn again. "Is there any way that I could be a better mother…that we could become closer?"

The look of puzzlement that now clearly swept across Susie's face, rapidly changing to a frown of confusion and annoyance, told Emma that, regardless of her precocity, the child was not capable of handling such large, abstract challenges and had never given a moment's thought to her relationship with her mother. What nine-year-old would?

Feeling foolish and ashamed, Emma rushed to Susie and hugged her.

"Never mind, Susie. Your mother's just in a strange mood. I guess all I'm saying is, you know I love you, right?"

"Sure, Mom," was her only reply, and Emma realized that this terse affirmation was all she was going to get from her daughter.

Emma laughed as she dismissed her silly notion of some extemporaneous heart-to-heart, probing discussion with Susie. She kissed Susie on her head and, releasing her, watched her disappear up the stairs. I am who I am, she thought, and she is who she is, even at nine, and our pattern is already set. In years to come, things might change but for now, let it be. Resigned to this recognition, Emma turned her attention back to preparing dinner.

With Jonathan and Jeremy, Emma had no more success. Except for animated dinner-table conversations when, with Emma's promptings, the two boys described their latest baseball, basketball or soccer game, or related a funny story about some teacher or fellow student, they behaved awkwardly when Emma made feeble attempts to participate more fully in their lives.

Oliver and the boys loved watching professional sports, in which Emma had no interest. When she tried to join this male circle, her endless questions about game rules or players clearly were testing the patience of both her husband and her sons. Likewise, in trying to show an interest in her boys' video games, Emma quickly saw that she was being politely tolerated.

Emma understood her sons well enough to know that, after her failed attempt with Susie, no verbal trial balloon about her effectiveness as a mother could be floated before Jonathan and Jeremy. She also recognized that, except for a usual, quick hug before the morning school bus approached, and an equally grazing, routine hug before bed, no new demonstrations of motherly affection would be received without embarrassment. She settled for furtively tousling their hair in passing.

Resolving to be alert to any new opportunities for greater participation in her children's lives, Emma consoled herself with thoughts of the good, strong character that each child was developing and quickly reverted to her usual pattern with them in her daily life. Yet she was acutely aware that the parental role that Oliver filled instinctively, she had to play consciously, and she wondered if this was a legacy from her parents.

20

Oliver had recently completed a sprawling post-modern house set on twenty acres of rolling land, overlooking a large pond, for George and Michelle Heredy. George owned a large chain of bowling alleys spread across several Midwestern states. Michelle was his second wife, fifteen years his junior and a former Miss Chicago, now a doting mother of four young children but still in great shape. In addition to designing the house, Oliver had been asked to supervise its construction for an additional hefty fee.

Except for a few of his old-money clients who treated all their paid professional contacts—doctors, lawyers, architects, psychotherapists and investment advisors—like domestic servants, most of his newly rich clients were so invested in, and excited about, the creation of their unique homestead that they came to consider Oliver as almost one of their family. The Heredys were no exception.

When the house was completed, including a two-lane bowling alley in the basement, a movie theater and an indoor-outdoor swimming pool, the interior designers and landscape architects took over. But Oliver, with his forceful personality, rugged good looks and that Princeton architectural degree, exuded such magnetism over people like the Heredys, who had made a lot of money but doubted their own taste, that they called on him to render an opinion on every ongoing aspect of the developing home.

When everything was finished, the proud owners, forgetting conveniently that it was mostly their money and not their discriminating taste that had created what they considered a masterpiece of the domestic arts, wanted to share their achievement with the world. They threw a lavish, catered party for friends, neighbors, business contacts, distant relatives and casual acquaintances they wanted to impress.

At some point in the festivities, George Heredy called for silence and gave unmitigated praise to Oliver for his "sheer genius, his creativity, his patience, his attention to every detail and his calmness in the face of setbacks and frustrations caused by our last-minute requests for changes in the plan."

"Remember, you still can't walk on water...not yet, anyway," Emma jovially reminded her husband as they walked to their car from this extravaganza, but she knew her husband was well grounded and took all this praise in stride.

"How I was able to accomplish all the endless changes they wanted after construction started might convince me that I could walk on water," Oliver quipped, and they both laughed.

While the closeness felt by most of Oliver's happy homeowners for their architect usually diminished to an occasional cocktail party invitation—always a source of potential clients Oliver had to remind a reluctant Emma—and an elaborate Christmas card, the Heredys were different.

George Heredy had graduated from a technical high school and had actually worked in a bowling alley before becoming part owner of it and starting his shrewd business climb to becoming a very rich man. Upon earning the title bestowed on him by the newspapers as The Bowling King of the Midwest, he had left his first wife, his high school sweetheart, and their two teenage children with a hefty settlement, when he met Michelle, a former beautician and newly minted Miss Chicago and fourth runner-up for Miss Illinois in the Miss U.S.A. pageant.

Unlike other clients who, having unexpectedly achieved some measure of success and recognition, immediately assume airs that they hope are commensurate with their new status, George and Michelle were the "salt-of-the-earth" types. While reveling in their newly found riches, they remained exactly who they were prior to their success, with no pretense, no facades. If you admired anything in their home or on their estate, they would tell you immediately what it cost, from both a sense of innocent wonderment at their own wealth and a desire to impress.

"Our Midwest version of the Beverly Hillbillies," Oliver had once described them to Emma before she met them at the house-warming party. Sure enough, they fit that description.

"Did you hear that, George?" Michelle had called to her husband across their crowded living room during the unveiling party. "Emma studied Greek and Latin in college. Can you beat that?" Turning back to Emma with a loud chuckle, she said, "Honey, I had enough trouble with English in high school."

"But you speak the language of love, babe, like an expert," George said, having crossed the room and now hugging his wife from behind. Michelle, who was at least three inches taller than her husky, balding husband in her stiletto heels, blushed, bringing color to her naturally pale Scandinavian skin up to the roots of her pale blond hair, arranged in an elaborate coiffeur. She had large, vivid green eyes, set off by heavy eye makeup, and a curved, ripe mouth. Emma marveled at her slim, curvaceous body after having four children but then she remembered the elaborate exercise room in the finished basement and, eyeing George's incipient paunch, she assumed that Michelle was the user.

Since the house-warming party, Oliver and Emma had been invited to a series of events at the Heredy home: sit-down dinners for never fewer than ten; Fourth of July barbecue; a surprise birthday party for Michelle whose age was not disclosed; elaborate parties celebrating the birthdays of their four children, inviting the entire Granby family.

Some of the Heredys' invitations conflicted with previous commitments and a few were declined because either Oliver or Emma didn't feel up to all the noisy gaiety and the Heredys' rollicking sense of exuberant fun. But Jonathan and Jeremy loved the parties celebrating the Heredy children's birthdays. There were pony rides and one time an elephant hired for the afternoon from a traveling circus that, with trainer in tow, obediently lumbered around a section of the huge back yard with several squealing children perched on his back.

That year it was a circus motif, with clowns and acrobats and jugglers. "George hired almost the entire circus, except the big cats," Michelle explained to Emma when the Granby family arrived. "It would have been cheaper to take everyone to the performance." Then she laughed. "But this is more fun, don't you think?"

Oliver, with his practical eye for business, participated in the Heredys' revelry with indulgent bemusement. Emma, however, felt herself drawn to both George and Michelle for their unabashed happiness in finding themselves so well off, and their appealing candor in expressing their childlike glee for everything that their money could buy them.

Emma's friend and neighbor, Carol Mumford, whose husband managed George Heredy's investment portfolio, said, "With all the sedate manners and genteel airs of the people we normally interact with, it's a refreshing change to have the Heredys who are natural and honest and warm. Of course, most of our crowd refuses to have anything to do with them." Carol placed her finger at the tip of her nose and tilted it up. "Much too grand for the likes of the bowling alley king and his beauty-pageant wife," she said in an affected voice, dripping with condescension, while Emma laughed. "And the few who have accepted their invitations," Carol continued in her normal voice, "only go so they can regale their guests at their next dinner party with all the ghastly excesses of what they saw." Returning to her affected voice and tilting her head upward while lowering her eyelids, "So *nouveau riche*, darling! So totally *parvenu*! So outrageously amusing!"

Emma was mindful of this conversation when she next attended a dinner party at the Heredys' home with Oliver.

21

On entering the Heredys' imposing home, Emma was pleased to see Carol and her husband Gardner. With her impressive height, her striking angular face and her full mane of red hair, Carol always stood out. Of the twelve people gathered for cocktails before assembling around the massive circular dining table—Oliver, who had been consulted, always recommended a circular dining table for large spaces—Emma knew Harriet and Arthur Bixby from the club and had a very casual acquaintance with the two other couples, Bob and Beth Corwin and Dick and Lauren Hoffsteder, "our nice neighbors," as Michelle described the four of them in introducing everyone as they were standing in the spacious living room.

"We met at the house-warming party, Dick Hoffsteder announced while shaking hands with Oliver.

"Yes, you're the genius architect," Bob Corwin said, smiling broadly and making a sweeping gesture encompassing the room. Emma thought she detected a hint of mockery in his voice.

"You're really quite famous in these parts," Beth Corwin said quickly in a pleasant voice with a nervous edge, as if she, too, had detected a sarcastic hint in her husband's remark and was hastening to cover it up.

"And deservedly so!" Arthur Bixby said. "I've been in four or five homes that Oliver has designed, and each one is unique."

"We only wish we could afford you," Harriet Bixby, a small, self-effacing lady with sad eyes, said, rather too modestly, Emma thought. Arthur was a prominent lawyer in the city, and their house, while old, sat on a twenty-acre spread

"I'm cheaper than you think." Oliver quipped, and everyone laughed politely.

"No, he's not!" George Heredy said loudly. "He cost me a fortune but he's worth every penny of it." George showed his exuberance as a host by speaking in a very loud voice over all of his guests.

"We've always wanted to add two more bedrooms and expand our family room," Harriet Bixby said in a tiny voice, and then glanced nervously at her husband for his approval. Emma remembered that Carol had always referred to Harriet as "the little mouse."

"I'm offering a ten percent discount on home additions this month," Oliver said, continuing in the jocular vein, appropriate for the light chatter of the occasion.

"So take him up on his offer before it expires!" George Heredy bellowed from the elaborate bar at the far corner of the living room." More polite laughter. Emma remembered how Oliver had tried to dissuade George from putting a bar in his living room, suggesting it would be better placed in his den, his recreation room or even by the covered pool, George decided that he wanted one in each of those places including the living room.

Emma kept a frozen smile on her face but did not join in the banter. Her thoughts were already drifting away. She could predict the course of the remaining hour of the cocktail portion of the evening. The men would wander over to the bar area and tell a few risqué jokes in lowered voices not intended for their wives to hear. Then they'd move on to talking about business, the latest sports event viewed on their gigantic flat-screen TV sets, the Dow Jones average, their golf game and whatever hot political issues were in the news.

Being all staunch conservatives, they could vehemently share their views with no dissenting opinions. Emma recalled how ironic it seemed that George Heredy, the son of immigrants, the prototypical rags-to-riches boy, would always be the most outspoken of them all,

Meanwhile, the women, seated comfortably on the sofas arranged intimately around the sleek slate and steel fireplace, would remark politely on the hors d'oeuvres that were always served by Michelle's maid, Margarita, who looked remarkably like Inez in Emma's class. Then they would talk about children and school and perhaps indulge in some light gossip about people they discovered they knew in common. They, too, would discuss their golf games since most of them played golf, except for Emma and Carol and Michelle.

"Honey, I never could see why you'd want to spend almost the whole day hitting a little ball into a little hole. I'd rather go shopping," was Michelle's summary evaluation.

If the conversation lagged, they could always fill in the gaps with admiring statements about one another's dress, jewelry or new hairdo, and there were always the tried and true fallback topics of latest fashions, movie star gossip, newly discovered recipes and difficulties with help—usually said in the presence of Margarita who clearly looked embarrassed.

The cocktail hour progressed seamlessly as Emma foresaw. With due diligence she contributed her required amount of comments and observations to this pleasant but vapid ritual while working on automatic pilot, her mind wandering to the prison classroom and Mercy's health scare.

22

Mercy had appeared tired and sluggish for several weeks as she went about her routines as Emma's aide. With Emma's urging, Mercy reluctantly admitted that she had not been feeling well and would go the next day to see the prison doctor. That was on a Thursday, and when Emma arrived for her class the following Tuesday, she found Virginia Ryan waiting in the classroom for her.

"Mercy's been sent to the city hospital," Virginia announced in her typically direct style. "It could be serious," she added, a hint of compassion softening her tone.

Emma found herself responding to this news as though Mercy were a member of her family. The color quickly drained from her face and her mouth went slack. Her arms hung limply at her sides but her fists were clenched. She could feel the blood draining from her head and she had to sit down. She quickly slid into a seat at one of the student desks, the kind where the chair was attached to the desk, and looked expectantly at Virginia, waiting for more news.

"They found a large lump in her breast."

Emma heard the words that every woman fears and felt that all the air was being sucked out of her lungs. "On, no!" was all she said.

"The biopsy report won't be back from the lab for some time," Virginia added, "so until then we won't know for sure."

Emma saw a glimmer of hope.

"We shouldn't jump to the worst conclusions before we get the lab report," Virginia cautioned

"No," Emma agreed, with little conviction.

"In the meantime, I'll see if I can't get you a substitute aide."

"Please don't bother," Emma said optimistically. "I can manage until Mercy comes back. When do you think we might have the lab report?"

"It usually takes about two weeks," Virginia said. "They seem to take their time with prison samples, like these lives aren't as important as others."

"Really," Emma said, distressed further by Virginia's last statement. "Could I visit her?"

"No, Emma. That's against the rules," Virginia answered quickly. She saw Emma's visible disappointment and spoke in a sterner tone. "I know you value Mercy because she's been a great help to you, and, I grant you, she's a special lady, as you've told me often, but I hope you haven't formed a special attachment to her."

"No," Emma said, knowing that was a lie.

She had formed a very special emotional bond with Mercy. It wasn't just the tremendous help Mercy had been to her in helping Emma to organize the class. Mercy had generously shared her insights concerning the students and guided her through thorny patches with individual class members. In her quiet, soft spoken and cheerful way, Mercy had coached Emma and made her a much better teacher. Through Mercy's support and encouragement, Emma had gained confidence through those first months of teaching.

Emma knew that Mercy quietly did a lot of intervention behind the scenes with the women in the class that resulted in a much smoother operation. But it was during the half-hour preparation periods before each class—when Emma and Mercy were working and talking and Mercy would share stories about the inmates or about her hardscrabble life and her struggles with her children—that Emma came to see this woman's noble character and indomitable spirit.

For a while, Emma struggled with reconciling the warm, caring nature that Mercy consistently displayed with the one act of violence that had landed her behind bars. But as their time together lengthened, Emma's struggle with this conflict disappeared and she surrendered to Mercy's good heart and impressive strength.

Emma had also resolved, after a few more months in the classroom, that she would never judge any of the inmates, especially Mercy, but accept them as they presented themselves to her. This resolution had resulted in her feeling that a great burden had been lifted from her, and she saw her students with new appreciation.

Yes, she had to admit, she admired Mercy tremendously and felt a strong attachment with her.

23

As the cocktail chatter filled the air surrounding her, Emma's thoughts skipped ahead to next Tuesday when she hoped that Mercy's lab test results might finally be back. She was waiting anxiously to get some definite word, hoping for the best but dreading the worst.

Having drifted away from the conversation, Emma heard Carol ask, "Emma, are you okay? You look strange."

Retreating from her thoughts, Emma smiled at the inquisitive faces gazing expectantly at her and said, "I'm fine."

Now she tried to focus on the women's conversation until Margarita, the maid, told Michelle that dinner was ready, and the six couples trooped into the sleek, candle lit dining room. At this point, all usual topics of conversation had pretty much been exhausted, so the guests turned their attention to the food, exclaiming about its quality. The women kept up most of the chatter while the men concentrated on eating.

As coffee and dessert were being served, Dick Hoffsteder, seated on Emma's right, said, during a lull in the conversation, "My wife just told me that you do some kind of charity work at the women's prison."

"Yes," Emma replied, suddenly happy to talk about a subject of importance to her. "I teach a GED class."

From the other side of her husband, Lauren Hoffsteder asked, "What's that?"

"It prepares adults to get a high school equivalency diploma," Emma explained, smiling at the group.

Directly across the table, George Heredy, in a loud, sarcastic voice, said "You mean we send them to prison and then we offer them an education at taxpayers' expense?"

Emma's smile disappeared. From her left side she felt Oliver's knee pressing against hers, warning her to be cautious. She took a deep breath.

"It doesn't cost the taxpayers anything, George, except maybe a few school supplies, and a lot of those are donated. And, remember, I'm a volunteer." Emma made this declaration in what she hoped was a neutral voice.

Lauren Hoffsteder looked around the table, gave a short chuckle and said, "Why anyone would want to put themselves in that god-awful prison, surrounded by the worst elements, is beyond me."

"It takes a special person, Lauren, and Emma finds it very rewarding," Carol said, coming to her friend's defense.

"Maybe so," Lauren said, "but isn't it dangerous?"

"Not really," Emma said, struggling to keep her voice light. "I only deal with a total of eleven inmates, including my aide, and there's always a guard stationed outside my classroom door."

"I still say that prisoners, whether they're men or women, should not be coddled," George Heredy said emphatically. "Education courses and programs teaching them trades and crafts. They break the law and then they're sent away to places that are run like country clubs or vacation resorts."

"Have you ever seen the inside of a prison?" Carol asked.

"Only on television," George admitted.

"I assure you, George," Emma said, staring directly at her host, "they're not run like country clubs. And a five-by-eight- foot cell does not remotely resemble even the cheapest room at any vacation resort."

"They're not penal colonies; they're supposed to be rehabilitation centers," Carol added.

"But do they rehabilitate?" Dick Hoffsteder asked, addressing his question to the table.

"No," said Bob Corwin. "Not according to the recidivism rates."

"And why do you think they're so high?" Emma asked, with a growing tightness evident in her voice.

"Because those people are the dregs of society to begin with, and when you incarcerate all of them together, they only encourage one another to commit more crimes as soon as they're released," Bob Corwin said with conviction.

Emma had visibly winced at the expression, "those people," and now she felt the eyes of all her dinner companions were turning to her, waiting for a reply. She took a sip of her coffee before speaking.

"That could be one explanation for the high recidivism rates, Bob, but another explanation could be that these women, whom you describe as the dregs of society, never had an even chance in life to begin with. They are born in poverty, surrounded by crime-infested neighborhoods, often abused or neglected as children, and too readily seek love and security and affirmation with men who exploit their vulnerabilities and use them for their own criminal ends, whether it be prostitution or hiding drugs or accomplices in more violent crimes. Then, as you say, they're tossed in with the mentally unstable and some truly vicious characters and they struggle to survive in that harsh environment. When they're released, they must return to the same pernicious surroundings that left them unprotected and desperately needy in the first place. No money. No education. Little chance of a job with a prison record. Is it any wonder that the recidivism rate is so high? It should amaze us that it isn't higher. And, as a matter of fact, Bob, the recidivism rate for women who commit murder is extremely low because, unlike men who commit random acts of murder, women usually murder abusive men in their lives."

Emma realized that her tone had become harder and more sarcastic the longer she spoke, so she abruptly stopped and took another sip of coffee. From across the table George Heredy now spoke in his booming voice.

"Emma, you and Oliver are our good friends, but I must say that you sound like a typical bleeding-heart liberal, always making excuses for the poor, the downtrodden, the neglected." George slammed his fist on the table, causing the glasses in his vicinity to rattle. "I was born poor and came from a tough neighborhood and nobody gave me a handout. I went to work when I was thirteen and I made something of myself and now I have everything I could wish for in life, and if I can do it, anybody can."

Michelle Heredy, who, up to this point, had been listening to the conversation but not participating, now spoke. "From everything you've told me about your childhood, George, your tough neighborhood was not drug infested and you had parents who were poor but they loved their kids and looked out for them. They worked hard to give you and your seven brothers and sisters a decent home and food and clothes, and they set an example for you to work hard. And, George, I'm grateful to say that you weren't a woman."

Everyone laughed, even Emma.

"Don't you start, Michelle," George said, half in jest. "You're another bleeding-heart liberal!"

"If that means that I can sympathize with people who are worse off than I am, then, yes, I am" Michelle said with a jerk of her head.

"You had a hard life, too, and you made something of yourself," George said.

Michelle laughed. "From the time I was twelve, George, I had shapely legs, big boobs and a nice ass, and my mother had been pushing me into beauty pageants since I was six, when I was Little Miss Appleton Amusement Park. Smiling at all the surrounding faces, Michelle continued. "I was Little Miss Chiclets when I was seven and Little Miss Illinois at nine. I dropped out of high school to go to Beauty School so I could learn more about hair and make-up for my pageant competitions but also so when my pageant days were over, I would have a way of making a living.

Supportive smiles circled the table, quickly to fade into looks of confusion as Michelle added, "I had two abortions before I was twenty, thanks to men who I thought loved me but were total shits when the chips were down, and my sharp-eyed, ambitious mother convinced me that my pageant career came first." As though it were an afterthought, Michelle said, "George knew all about this when I married him."

Emma was the only one now sending a supportive smile to Michelle, in true admiration of this woman's honesty and openness. The rest were glumly silent until Carol spoke. "Can any woman at this table honestly say that they didn't feel secure and loved as children?"

"My parents were divorced when I was seven," Harriet Bixby announced, "but I knew they loved me and my two older brothers, and my Dad paid for all our college educations."

Polite murmurs of appreciation from around the table.

"I still say," George Heredy asserted with his typical pugnacity "that we all make choices in life and everybody has some hard-luck story, and those people who make the wrong choices and go outside the law deserve to be punished and we shouldn't coddle them."

"Do you really think the law is always fair and justice is always blind?" Emma asked.

"Yes, of course I do," George answered

"Then consider this case," Emma said, preparing to give a brief sketch of Inez, one of her Latino students. She saw that she had the attention of the entire table so she began.

"A young girl—let's call her Inez—is born into a dirt-poor family in Puerto Rico, the ninth child of eleven."

"There's the problem right there?" Dick Hoffsteder exclaimed. "They breed like rabbits and can't take proper care of their kids."

"But your president, Dick, outlaws contraception as a part of any aid program," Carol said, "and the Catholic Church forbids it, too."

No one responded.

"Besides," Emma said, "is it Inez's fault that she's born into a family that can't feed or clothe her properly?" No answer came from the listeners, and Emma continued. "Inez's two older sisters had left Puerto Rico for New York where they got jobs as house cleaners and, at first, were sending a little money back to the family but then the money stopped and the sisters wrote that the high cost of living took every penny they made. So Inez decides she'd like to join her sisters and maybe she could help her family a little. She's seventeen when she arrives in New York and finds her two sisters living in one room of a four-room apartment in a slum area where each of the rooms has been rented to a different family. She also finds that her sisters are addicted to crack cocaine and a man living in one of the other rooms—let's call him Reuben—is their supplier. They no longer work cleaning apartments but now are hookers, working for Reuben. Inez is horrified by everything she sees but within a week Reuben has raped her and soon she's following in her sisters' footsteps, smoking crack and turning tricks."

"That's where she made the wrong choice!" George Heredy shouted.

"Yeah, George, she really had a lot of options," Carol said with clear sarcasm. "She could have become a high fashion model or gone off to a convent, right?"

George made no response. Emma continued.

"One night Inez picks up an older man driving a Mercedes and takes him to a motel. Without telling Inez, Reuben and his two brothers follow her to the motel, break in and start shaking down the john. But the john is a retired army office and he resists and starts fighting all three brothers. Reuben shoots and kills the john. The motel manager sees Reuben breaking into the room and calls the police who come and arrest Inez, Reuben and his two brothers before they can get away. The three men now claim that Inez shot the john.

"What about fingerprints on the gun?" Arthur Bixby asked, interrupting Emma's narrative.

"They had been wiped off," Emma replied. "Now Reuben and his two brothers have been amassing a lot of money pimping a whole string of girls and selling drugs, and they can afford expensive, high-powered lawyers who get them off. But they do nothing for Inez, still insisting that she shot the man. Inez must rely on a public defender who advises her to plead guilty to manslaughter and throw herself on the mercy of the court. Alone, abandoned even by her two sisters who are totally dependent on Reuben, having no knowledge of our court system, she follows her lawyer's advice and gets a sentence of fifteen to twenty years."

Emma paused and glanced around the table.

"Doesn't this case history seem to you like a good illustration of big money equals big lawyers and lenient justice while no money equals overworked public defenders and harsh justice?"

"That's a typical sob story of a liberal," George Heredy said, smiling at Emma. "I bet every one of those people have a sob story."

"George, you keep saying 'those people,' like they were an alien race," Carol pointed out. "How come we don't see our wealthy corporate swindlers or big government officials getting long sentences when they're found guilty of white-collar crimes? That seems to me to be powerful evidence of unequal treatment by the law."

A few minutes earlier, Michelle Heredy had left the table and everyone assumed that she was going to the bathroom or to check on her children. Now she returned and walked over to where Emma was sitting

"Didn't you say that a lot of your school supplies were bought through donations?" she asked.

Surprised, Emma looked up and said "Yes."

"Well, I admire the work you're doing and I'd like to make a donation," Michele said in a defiant tone that seemed to be daring her husband to object, but George just shook his head, smiled indulgently and remained silent.

"Here!" Michelle said, thrusting a check at Emma who took the check and saw it was for five hundred dollars.

"That's very generous, Michelle. Thank you," Emma said, squeezing her hostess's hand.

"That's my wife!" George shouted, benignly amused. "She spends it faster than I can make it!"

Michelle ignored her amused husband and said, "Just a small gift from one bleeding heart to another. Let me know if you need more."

Carol, who always enjoyed a dramatic flourish and tweaking the noses of socially conservative peers, spoke up. "Whatever that amount is, Emma, I'll match it." Looking straight at her host, she added, "And I'm not spending my husband's money, am I, George?" A reminder that Carol was probably the independently wealthiest person in the room.

The people around the table laughed nervously since the conversation had taken on a combative tone that was unexpected.

Michelle said, "Now how about some after-dinner drinks and some cards in the game room?"

The diners left the table quickly, happy to escape the increasingly tense atmosphere. They had stumbled into areas that violated the code of polite, frivolous dinner conversation and were eager to resume the façade of amiable chatter.

24

It had been a taxing evening and Emma felt tired. She was grateful when she heard Oliver pleading an early-morning meeting with a client as the reason for an early departure.

"Another Granby masterpiece!" George boomed as he and Michelle escorted them to the front door. "Okay, we'll let you go this time, but don't be strangers. We expect to see you soon." George was again filled with boisterous good humor and he gave Emma a bear hug and said, "Besides my wife, you're my favorite bleeding-heart liberal," and she knew he meant it. She reminded herself that he hadn't objected to Michelle's check; yet, he had a typically narrow, biased view about "those people." Still, she liked this man, who was far more honest in expressing his views than a lot of people who, she knew, held the same views secretly.

Once they were in the car and heading home, Emma was lost in thought. She gazed out the window at all the fine large houses perched on large, rolling plots of land with beautifully manicured lawns, thinking that all the inhabitants, snug in their wealthy cocoons, smug in their social positions and secure in their place in the world, had little understanding of, or appreciation for, how others—a huge number of "those people"—were living and struggling and being knocked down by overwhelming odds. She acknowledged that she, too, had been smug and blinded to the harsh realities of other lives until her eyes were opened through her students and especially through Mercy, who had taught her to have a compassionate heart.

This gathering tonight, she thought, was like so many dinner parties that she and Oliver had attended through the years, as groups of like-minded people reveled in the tacit acknowledgment of their financial and social achievements.   She suddenly remembered the short story, *The Masque of the Red Death* by Edgar Alan Poe, in which a group of people, sequestered behind high walls to isolate themselves from the virulent plague that raged throughout the city, partied ferociously, indifferent to what was happening outside until the plague's contagion swooped over the wall and down on them.   We're like that group of revelers, she reflected, indifferent behind our facades, our walls and hedges and fences.   We drink and eat and chatter away about nothing, self-congratulatory in our nicely comfortable lives.

She flashed back to her own upbringing and her parents, surrounded by their graduate students, discoursing on literature and philosophy and politics and art.   So vastly different from...

Emma's thoughts were interrupted when Oliver, who had been silent to this point, said "You sounded pretty defensive tonight, Emma."

"That's because I was put on the defensive," she said quickly, realizing the irony of how easily she was again sounding defensive in her response to her husband.   "I didn't bring the subject of my prison volunteer work up, if you'll remember," she continued, "but when Dick Hoffsteder brought it up and then everyone jumped on the bandwagon, condemning *those people*, I was not about to sit there and politely take all the crap!"

"I'm not saying that your response was wrong or inappropriate," Oliver said in a low, calm voice, "but if every party we attend is going to turn into a debate on social issues, I think we'll wear out our welcome pretty fast."

"You mean *I'll* wear out my welcome," Emma shot back, looking at her husband's profile through the shadows in the car. "I didn't hear a word from you on either side."

Oliver uttered a short sigh before responding. "Emma, I don't attend these parties to bare my soul or make lifelong friends or even to have a particularly good time. George Heredy is a lovable, laughable goofball who's made a hell of a lot of money and who gladly and promptly pays any commission I charge him for my work. He's proud of the house I designed for him and wants to show it off and, in case you forgot, that has already led to two new clients and possibly a third. My business is such that I'm dependent on the good will and good word of my customers, and that word is spread through social occasions such as tonight's. That's why I go and that's why I keep it light and that's why I get the hell out as soon as I can."

"That's fine, Oliver," Emma said, clipping her words, her anger rising. "I'll play the dutiful wife, taking part in all the superficial conversations so we can make a good impression and you can get more clients. But please understand that if I'm ever challenged about my volunteer work and about my sympathies for *those people*, I will respond as strongly and, as you say, defensively as I did tonight—your clients be damned!"

"Spoken like the staunch liberal you seem to have become," Oliver said with a commingling of surprise and teasing in his voice. She could always count on Oliver to deflate her rising anger with a conciliatory gesture or a funny, slanted remark, and now she found herself suddenly smiling.

"Yes, I guess you're right," she said in a much lighter tone, "And right in the bosom of your family. But speaking of liberals, I remember there was a time when a certain young architect, fresh out of Princeton, wanted to build beautiful houses and make a lot of money but also wanted to do volunteer work for Habitat for Humanity. What ever happened to him?"

Oliver took one hand off the wheel and reached over to squeeze hers. "He got lost somewhere along the way, I guess," he said, and she thought she detected both resignation and regret in his voice. She returned his squeeze.

"It's not too late," she said brightly.

He didn't respond and they drove through the dark night in silence as she thought about how much she had changed and how far she had come in the brief time that she had been working in the prison and had been exposed to Mercy. "Things aren't always what they seem," was Mercy's favorite comment. She had been mostly content to look upon the surface features of her comfortable, secure life and not question the values underpinning it. But through Mercy, she had expanded her perspective to embrace other, harsher realities. With this new awareness came greater empathy and deeper understanding—so much so that she now found the normal boundaries of her social class to be suffocating.

It's not that these people aren't decent and reasonable, she admitted to herself. They abide by the law, raise families, go to church, give to charities and think of themselves as upstanding examples of real Americans. But when it comes to social issues and minorities and justice, they are blind. They don't want to hear about *those people*.

Emma had arrived at a place where she felt totally separate from them. She loved her husband and her children—that was a constant—but her blinders were off and she could not go back. New adjustments between Oliver and her would have to be negotiated and new agreements understood. She was hopeful but resolved.

25

The following Tuesday, Emma arrived at the prison earlier than usual, eager to visit Virginia Ryan's office to get news of Mercy's lab tests' results.

John Cooper was the guard on duty at the entrance gate, and Emma smiled when she saw him. John was one of the few guards who interacted with the visitors. A huge African-American man in both height and girth, John always had a smile for everyone, as his chin disappeared into the folds of his massive neck.

Visiting days were usually on the weekend and the inmates' last names were split A to L and M to Z for alternate weekends. With special permission, families could visit during the week.

In front of Emma as she passed through the main gate was an older African-American woman with two young children, a boy and a girl, whom Emma judged to be about three and five. The kids were dressed in their Sunday best and the little girl's hair was arranged in several pigtails with ribbons. Both children looked nervous, clearly intimidated by the formidable iron gate and the austere surroundings of the inspection hall. Emma watched as John approached them with his wide open-mouth grin and a massive chuckle.

"Well, now, look who has come to visit us: the prettiest girl and the handsomest boy I've seen in a long time." The girl smiled awkwardly and her little brother looked up at the huge smiling man with a mixture of curiosity and awe. "And who are you visiting today?" John asked as though this were very important news to him. The little girl rocked from side to side. "My mama," she said shyly.

"And what a lucky mama she is to have such beautiful children." John said, patting both children on the head with his mammoth hands. "What's your name, honey?"

Looking up at the lady she was with—Emma guessed it was her grandmother—the girl, in a tiny voice, said "Shirell,"

"What a pretty name for such a pretty girl!" John exclaimed, and Shirell beamed. John turned his attention to the little brother. "And what's your name?" The boy's hands flew to his mouth and he backed up into his grandmother. "His name is Jordan," Shirell said, "after Michael Jordan."

All visitors had to be inspected, even children. Mercy had told Emma of a sister of one of the inmates who had tried to smuggle a cell phone into the prison in a baby's diaper. Most of the guards were indifferent to how frightening the inspection process could be to young children, but John Cooper made a game of it. Still grinning from ear to ear, he picked the little boy up and placed him, standing, on the inspection table. He showed the boy the metal detecting wand.

""You know what, Jordan? I've got a magic wand here that tells me if you've been a good boy." The child's big brown eyes inspected the wand closely. "And if you have been a good boy, the wand will tell me and then you get a piece of candy. Would you like that?"

Still fascinated with the wand, the boy managed a faint smile and shook his head up and down.

"So here we go now. Stand up straight. Can you hold your arms out like this?" John extended his long arms straight out from his sides. "My magic wand wants to be sure that you've been a good boy." Clearly caught up in the spell that John was casting, the boy's smile broadened and he extended his arms in imitation of John's. "Okay, here comes the magic wand. Close your eyes, Jordan, and think of candy."

Giggling now, the boy followed John's instructions and his body swayed slightly as John quickly moved the wand around the contours of the boy's body.

"Very good so far," John said, and the boy opened his eyes. "But there's one more test." John picked the boy up and sat him on the table. "If you've really been very, very good, my magic wand will tell me after looking at your toes."

The boy, totally absorbed in John's fantasy, shook his shoulders and giggled some more as John quickly removed the child's shoes and unobtrusively ran his fingers around the inside, making certain that nothing was concealed there. All visitors, regardless of age, had to remove their shoes, like at the airport security inspection. With a dramatic gesture John brought the wand close to the boy's toes.

"The magic wand is telling me that you've been a very good boy,"

John slipped the child's shoes back on and placed him back on the floor. He produced a piece of wrapped hard candy from a bulging side pocket of his pants. "And here's your reward for being so good," he said, like the MC on a television show announcing to the contestant that he had won the grand prize. The boy's body was squirming with delight as he eagerly took the candy from John's baseball-mitt hand and looked at his grandmother. She smiled and nodded her head and the boy quickly unwrapped the candy and, handing the wrapper back to John, popped it into his mouth.

John turned to the little girl who had been watching everything with eyes wide with fascination.

"Are you ready for the magic wand, Shirell?   John asked in his booming voice and the little girl eagerly shook her head.

Emma watched as John repeated his magic routine and when he was finished with the child, she, too, enjoyed her candy. John continued the charade by telling the children that even their grandmother would be inspected by the magic wand and she, too, earned a piece of candy.   Happy and relaxed, thanks to the kindness of this thoughtful guard, the family left the inspection center to visit the children's mother.

So many of the guards, Emma reflected, both men and women, were performing their job with complete indifference to the inmates and, except for barking orders or shouting warnings, no personal exchange ever took place, underscoring further the dehumanizing elements of prison life. The small minority of the guards who, by word or gesture, treated the women with a modicum of respect were doubly appreciated. Yet, they, too, were opening themselves to possible trouble, in danger of having the hardened, exploitative inmates "get over" them with some scheme or other.

Mercy had frequently reminded Emma that for every inmate that was a simple soul betrayed by a loved one, there were other, darker souls who had willingly and thoroughly embraced a criminal life and were always looking to exploit the weak, the soft, the compassionate. Mercy told Emma a story of one such inmate who cajoled a young female guard into making a private call on the inmate's behalf to the inmate's boyfriend. Later, it was discovered that the message the inmate had written out for the guard to deliver on the phone, while appearing innocent on the surface, was a coded instruction about sneaking drugs into the prison. So the warning to guards and volunteers about keeping their distance from inmates was warranted, and the penalties for violating the rules could be severe—the young female guard had been fired— but the necessary result was a cold, sterile environment in which inmates were constantly made aware of their inferior, stigmatized status.

In Emma's mind, Mercy was clearly an exception—one of the good souls who had made one egregious mistake—and Emma had warmed to Mercy right away, enjoying her gentle guidance and warm personality in the classroom and their shared stories before and after class. Emma liked most of her students, too, but, thanks to Mercy's promptings, was wary of letting down her guard. Only with Mercy was she entirely relaxed and confidential, and in their relationship she accepted responsibility for knowingly violating the rules.

As John approached her for the inspection, she smiled and said, "You certainly have a wonderful way with kids, John."

John laughed. "I've got five of my own, so it comes natural." He paused and looked away. "And the kids didn't break the law, their mama did."

And yet, Emma thought, the kids are made to suffer, too.

26

Having completed the routine inspection with John, who always greeted her cheerfully, Emma hurried along the corridor to Virginia Ryan's office. The door to the office was closed and Emma could hear voices inside, so she sat on the metal bench in the corridor and nervously waited for the door to open. After about five minutes, which in Emma's heightened anxiety seemed like fifty, the door opened and a woman whom Emma did not know exited down the hall. Emma stood n the doorway and asked "Any news about Mercy?"

"Come in, Emma, and close the door" Virginia said in a tone that instantly alarmed Emma. Virginia waited until Emma was seated before speaking. "I'm afraid the news isn't good."

"Oh," was all Emma could think of to say, as her throat constricted. She wanted to close her eyes and shut out Virginia's voice and this scene, and when she'd open them again she would be in her classroom with Mercy, doing their normal routines in preparation for the class, enjoying that quiet intimacy of two good friends. Instead, she stared fixedly at Virginia's desk, like some criminal awaiting sentencing.

"It's cancer," was the terse announcement Virginia made, always economizing on words, in her typically flat voice, but this time, shaded, too, with a darker tone suggesting pity. Emma visibly flinched but kept staring at the desk, trying mightily not to betray the powerful sense of shock and sorrow she was feeling. From some mysterious place inside her, a wellspring of hope gushed up to the surface of her brain. "Chances of recovery are very good with breast cancer, aren't they?" Emma asked, her voice edgier now, as she looked up from the desk and stared at Virginia, searching for confirmation of this hope.

Now it was Virginia whose eyes darted down to her desk. "If it's caught in time, yes," she said, "but Mercy's cancer is in an advanced stage and has already spread to her lymph nodes. She must have been suffering for a long time and never said anything or went to see the doctor."

Each word that Virginia uttered was like a stone falling on Emma's heart until she felt so weighted down that she couldn't move. She felt the tears lapping at the corners of her eyes.

"But there's still a chance of recovery, isn't there?" she said, pleading with Virginia to leave her some vestige of hope.

"Yes, there's always a chance," Virginia said, casually throwing Emma a lifeline. "She's scheduled to be operated on in the next few days and then we'll know more."

"When can I visit her?" Emma asked, struggling to regain control of her voice.

"You can't," was Virginia's instant reply. Emma's face now expressed surprise and shock. "No one is allowed to visit inmates in the hospital except immediate family," Virginia said in her back-to-business tone.

"But Mercy doesn't have any family except her two daughters, and one is in a rehabilitation program in California and the other has cut off all communication with her mother," Emma said, the words tumbling out in a fusillade of indignation.

Virginia stared hard at Emma. "Those are the rules, Emma. There's nothing you or I can do about it."

Emma returned Virginia's stare, her desperation fueling her audacity.

"Given the fact that Mercy's been an honor inmate all these years and has no one to support her, can't someone in authority make an exception and let me see her?"

"No," Virginia said flatly, "and I'll tell you why. Your request would indicate that you've violated the prohibition against forming bonds with prisoners, and the superintendent would certainly not endorse your friendship with Mercy by letting you see her."

Emma felt cornered, desperate. She returned Virginia's even stare and her voice registered defiance. "We're not talking about bonds or friendship. This is a matter of common decency...of charity. How can we let this good woman suffer alone?"

"Common charity is not a virtue practiced much in prisons, Emma, and this good woman, as you call her, is a murderer. Let's not forget that."

"Oh God, Virginia, I never expected this from you!" Emma cried, crumbling in defeat.

Virginia rose, came around her desk and put her hand on Emma's shoulder. She spoke in a soft voice. "I don't mean to be harsh, but, Emma, it's very clear that you have formed a bond with Mercy and I warned you about that. I'm not saying Mercy isn't an exceptional person and sometimes, when I consider all her exemplary behavior throughout her years in prison, I wonder how she could have killed her daughter's boyfriend, even though she said she did. But the prison rules are based on reason and experience. We've had volunteers and guards who have been conned, or *got over* as the inmates say, and they've been sucked into being accomplices to serious prison violations or even crimes. I can understand how easily you and Mercy bonded, but that bond can't be acknowledged in any way. Can you understand that?"

Numbly, Emma shook her head, yes. Another iron gate had been slammed shut, with Mercy on one side and Emma on the other, and no one was going to unlock it for them.

"Will her daughter be notified?" Emma asked, with a final shudder of resignation, gazing off into space.

"Of course," Virginia said, patting Emma's shoulder. "I'll keep you posted as soon as I hear anything."

Emma silently rose and left the office, forgetting to say goodbye. She walked to her classroom in a daze, gripped by raw emotions. On entering her classroom she half expected to see Mercy, sitting quietly in a student desk in the rear of the room, arranging workbooks or recording test grades. She could see Mercy's large brown eyes sweeping over Emma in a warm appraisal and her luminous smile welcoming the teacher to this sealed-off little world where they were not prisoner and volunteer but, for a brief time, caring friends, sharing private thoughts, giving encouraging praise and relishing their laughter.

Emma sat down at her desk and now gave herself the liberty to cry. Her tears rippled down her cheeks, as she muffled her involuntary sobs with her hands. She knew she was not crying for Mercy alone or for her own sense of loss, but for all the women whose stories had touched and expanded her; for all the deep sadness and bleak expectations or utter despair that permeated these prison confines, as palpable as the prison bars and walls and locks—a shrinking of the human heart and the shriveling of life, itself.   No one noticed; no one cared; after all, it was just *those people.*

This, she thought, is what John Milton meant in *Paradise Lost* when he described Hell as "darkness visible."

PART THREE

27

Her eyes rimmed with a dark red glow from tears and hand rubbing, Emma was superficially composed when her students arrived for class. Some of them knew already that Mercy was in the hospital—news traveled by mysterious channels in prison with a speed that outpaced any website connection—but did not know the diagnosis. Emma did not share this information with her students, who were clearly upset and needed to talk.

For the next fifteen minutes that Emma allowed before cutting off conversation, she heard many stories of kindness, helpfulness, guidance and thoughtfulness that most members of the class had experienced with Mercy. Several women spoke about Mercy's offers to help them, during the evening recreation time, with those parts of the GED curriculum that they found the most challenging.

In the Day Room where the inmates from specific cell blocks were allowed to gather, when not scheduled for work or some other daily routine, to watch television and socialize, Mercy stationed herself at an empty table at the far end of the room from where most of the women gathered and offered one-on-one tutorials to the women in Emma's class. Others spoke about her as a sympathetic ear, always willing to listen to their troubles and generously giving her sound advice or consoling words. Small acts of kindness were mentioned, as were thoughtful gestures like hand-written birthday cards to each member of the class—Emma realized she didn't know their birthdays and had never thought of this.

"She always signed them with your name and hers, but we knew they were from her." Helen said with her typical sarcastic edge, as though she were reading Emma's mind.

"And she never had nobody come to visit her," Inez said, and the other women shook their heads in sympathetic unison. ""She got two daughters but they never visit."

"But she always had a smile for everybody," said Columbia, a stout, African-American who was usually quiet and seldom spoke.

Emma smiled appreciatively at all the students' praise of Mercy, but she was also smiling inwardly at their unvarnished testament to Mercy's compassionate heart. Their words were a thorough validation of her own intuitive appraisal of Mercy's character.

"When I was tryin' to write my appeal," Columbia said, all shyness having disappeared, "Mercy helped me any time I axt her."

Emma flashed back to another scene with Mercy who had shared Columbia's story when Emma noticed that Columbia seemed not just shy but depressed and withdrawn in class.

"Columbia had three kids by the time she was twenty-one by a man named Caleb who was no good," Mercy had explained, the sides of her mouth turning down in a disapproving frown. "He was always in trouble with the law, in and out of jail and never giving Columbia any help with the kids. She finally decides that she's better off without him. Then, after disappearing for months, he comes to her door and asks Columbia to take him back. Well, she was silly and he sweet-talked his way back into her heart."

Emma remembered the rest of the sad story. Caleb had suggested that they go away for a weekend, just the two of them, and leave the kids with Columbia's mother. She agreed and off they went to some motel in the country. He said he was going for a pack of cigarettes and some gas and left her in the motel.

Caleb drove his beat-up old truck to the nearest gas station where he saw that no one was there except some old guy running the place and he decided to rob him. He had a gun hidden in his truck and he pulled it on the old man who was behind the counter of the little store that was part of the gas station. Now the old guy was feisty and Caleb saw him reaching for something behind the counter and shot and killed him.

Caleb grabbed the money from the cash register and rushed back to his truck. He was speeding out of the station just as a car was pulling in. The driver was the brother of the old man, coming to take over for him. He was immediately suspicious of the way Caleb's tires were screeching as he flew out of the station and wrote down Caleb's license plate number. Then he discovered his dead brother in the store and called the sheriff and gave him the license plate.

In a little while, the sheriff found Caleb's truck parked outside the motel and stormed the room with some deputies and arrested Caleb. Caleb swore he was innocent and this was a frame-up of a black man for a white man's death. Columbia believed him and, to support her man, she went with him to the jail where the brother saw her and claimed she was in the cab of the truck with Caleb.

Both Caleb and Columbia swore that she was not in the truck, but they were both tried for murder—Columbia as an accessory—and the brother was the only witness and he testified that Columbia was in the truck. Her lawyer tried to discredit the brother by showing that he's near-sighted and doesn't wear glasses. Her lawyer also got the brother to admit that he used to be a member of the Klan when he lived in Georgia. But the jury disregarded these facts and Caleb's testimony that Columbia wasn't involved, and came back with a guilty verdict, and the judge sentenced Columbia to twelve-to-fifteen years.

Columbia enters prison and is a model prisoner, helped by a strong religious faith. She never gets into trouble because she wants to get out and take care of her kids. After eight years she's up for parole.

In order to grant parole, the review panel wants to hear the prisoner say she's sorry for what she did. They ask Columbia if she's sorry and she says, 'How can I be sorry for somethin' I don't do.?' So they deny her parole. Then her mother dies and her kids are sent to foster homes and she wants to get out in the worst way but she refuses to say she's sorry every time she comes up for parole. No matter how hard she tries to explain why she can't, the panel always denies her parole.

"Now her appeal just got turned down and that's why she's so down-hearted," Mercy had explained.

Mercy had concluded her story with a half-smile and a few more words, encouraging Emma to be understanding if Columbia seemed distracted. Emma never forgot that story and felt tremendous respect for Columbia's principled refusal, reminding herself that she would probably not have been so resolute when faced with the prospect of more years in prison and continued separation from her children.

The parole board insisted on open contrition, and this poor, uneducated black woman had shown the noblest courage in maintaining her innocence at the price of her freedom. It reminded Emma again of Mercy's often quoted observation: "Things aren't always what they seem."

Emma had reflected that it probably appeared to others that Columbia was being pigheaded and, in view of the horrendous consequences of her stubbornness, should have compromised for the sake of her children. But Emma had come to an appreciation of this woman's simple heart. To tell this lie meant the loss of the only things she had left: her dignity and unswerving belief in justice in the eyes of God.

Now here was Columbia joining the chorus of praises for Mercy.

Emma was deeply moved.

28

At the next writing session, most of the women were writing about Mercy. Anita, a gum-chewing, loud Latina woman in her twenties who was an active participant in class discussions, had been thinking about Mercy and her long trip to the nearest hospital, some sixty miles away, for her biopsy. Anita had been taken to the same hospital for a stomach tumor several years ago—she was serving a ten-to-twelve year involuntary manslaughter sentence for killing her common-law husband while defending herself from his sudden attack.

Emma knew Anita's history from Mercy, and in Anita's writings she had added rich details that allowed Emma to recall vividly the entire story.

Anita had hit him on the temple with an iron pot when he came home from the local bodega where he drank and played dominoes all day, since losing his job as a janitor in a factory two months earlier, for drinking on the job. He walked into the kitchen where she was standing in front of the stove, stirring the chicken and rice dish she had prepared earlier and was now reheating when he hadn't arrived home at their usual mealtime. She heard him come in and she said hello without turning toward him. He came up behind her—the strong smell of liquor filled her nostrils—and screamed that his supper should be on the table. Then he hit her on the side of her head with such force that she lost her balance and crashed to the floor, still holding the iron pot, with the chicken and rice streaming across the floor.

There was an instant ringing in her ears and her vision was blurred. She felt a blow to her side followed by a sharp pain. He was kicking her. The sight of her on the floor, surrounded by the spilled food enraged him further and he straddled her body, punching her wildly in the face and neck and head, all the while screaming insults.

She felt consciousness slipping away and knew that he would not stop. In one desperate move to save herself, one adrenalin-rushed summoning of strength, she swung her arm up from the floor, still holding the empty iron pot, and blindly, wildly struck him.

All action ceased. A silence, deafening in its uncertainty, surrounded her. Then his upper body crumpled into hers. Fearful that this was some new form of attack, she closed her eyes, unable to move, all her energy spent, resigned to almost certain death.

When nothing happened in the next few seconds, she became conscious of her breathing and almost simultaneously realized that his face, only inches to the side of hers, was soundless. Another few seconds passed and she felt a warm liquid lapping at the back of her head. Finally, she dared to turn her head toward her husband's face and saw the steady trickle of blood oozing from his temple and ear, forming a deep red bank leading to her head.

She screamed and pushed him off of her and then, rising to her knees, she huddled over him and saw that he wasn't breathing. At that moment, her husband's brother, who was living with them, came home from work and, entering the kitchen, heard her loud scream before she passed out in the widening pool of blood.

Anita's public defender reported to the court that she had been beaten many times by her boyfriend—the judge, displaying a petty, condescending prudery at the outset of the trial, instructed the lawyers to refer to Anita's husband as her boyfriend, since no marriage ceremony, he asserted, had sanctioned their union in the eyes of the law, thereby diminishing the defendant's status further in the eyes of the jurors as immigrant *and* harlot.

The prosecuting attorney had asked if these alleged previous beatings had ever been reported to the police—an action so alien to Anita's cultural code of conduct that, of course, the answer was "No." However, she told her lawyer that her husband's brother had witnessed a number of the beatings.

This younger brother, wishing to preserve his dead brother's honor, denied that he had ever seen any abuse and, to further polish his brother's reputation, asserted that it was Anita who had a violent temper, exacerbated by heavy drinking. The jury could now regard her as an immigrant, a harlot a liar and a drunk.

Anita's lawyer called the owner of the bodega which the boyfriend-husband had made a second home since losing his job. This man, fearful of the law and not having a license to sell anything except beer, while clandestinely selling cheap liquor to known clients under the counter, swore that he had never seen the boyfriend, a permanent fixture at the dominoes table outside the bodega, even mildly drunk.

Anita's jury deliberated less than an hour before bringing back a verdict of manslaughter, and a sentence of eight-to-ten years was quickly imposed.

Anita now read to the class about her experience in being transferred to the hospital for her pre-op visit.

"Two guards tie me up, my hands and feet, and put me in a van. When we get to hospital I have trouble walking and start to fall down but the guards hold me up. They take me to large room with lots of people looking sick. We go there at ten-thirty in the morning. I have metal chains around my hands and legs. Everybody look at me. I want to hide. I was very shamed. I want to die. The guards keep the chains on my ankles and take the chains from my hands. We sit in the room until four-thirty. When all the sick people leave, I see the doctor.

Emma listened to Anita's vivid description of her visit to the hospital, picturing the gentle, dignified Mercy in shackles, subjected to the world's condemning stares, forced to be on public display for hour after hour while other patients were seen and then Mercy was taken as the last—the least important—patient. By the time Anita finished reading her description of the hospital visit, Emma was rigid with indignation.

29

The following Tuesday, upon Emma's arrival at the prison, the guard at the inspection center looked at her ID badge and told her to go see Virginia Ryan. Emma walked quickly along the long corridor leading to Virginia's office, but before she got there she spotted Virginia walking briskly toward her. Virginia halted Emma's progress by placing both her hands on Emma's shoulders, as if to steady her.

"Emma, the news is bad." Virginia said, and her voice sounded softer than Emma had ever heard it. Emma's eyes darted from Virginia's grim face, trying to avoid the inevitable news. Virginia said no more, only took Emma's arm and led her to the office where she closed the door and practically pushed the anxious Emma into a chair. With her typical but not unkind forthrightness, Virginia got right to the point.

"The doctors have now found that Mercy's cancer has spread to her blood stream and her bone marrow. By the time she went to the doctor, it was too late."

Emma was staring at Virginia's lips, watching the words being formed as though she were watching a silent movie, while her brain fought, first to deny and then to comprehend, the words she was hearing: "blood stream…bone marrow…too late."

Emma was on intimate terms with cancer. Her mother had died a slow, agonizing death from pancreatic cancer, and less that two years after that, her father had died of prostate cancer. Now, from the corners of her memory she was hearing those ominous, hated words that, she knew, left not a sliver of hope to shatter the black horizon. It was hopeless and terminal and staggering in its simple projection.

"How long?" Emma asked, more from instinct than any active thought process.

"Not long, I understand," Virginia replied.

"Where is she now?"

"She's been brought back here to our medical unit."

"Can I see her?"

"Emma, you know the rules: only family members can visit a patient in the medical unit."

"Even under these extraordinary circumstances?" Emma pleaded, her voice a mixture of disbelief and indignation.

"Yes, I'm afraid so," Virginia said firmly.

"Can I send her flowers at least?" Emma asked, desperate to find some means of comforting Mercy.

Virginia now spoke like a patient mother. "If anyone in the medical unit saw the flowers were from you, they could report you and you'd be barred from the prison for violating the rule about a volunteer forming a bond with an inmate."

Emma stood up and her words now came with an explosive force that startled both her and Virginia.

"My God, Virginia, the hell with all this *special bond* bullshit! We're talking about a woman who's dying, and she's dying alone! She's not some throw-away object, like an old dishrag, to be disposed of without a thought. She's a human being—and, yes, a damn fine human being, even if she did commit murder. That's one minute among millions of minutes in her lifetime, as you once reminded me, and she shouldn't be judged by that one minute alone. Someone has to acknowledge her worth! Consideration must be given her!"

Her anger and frustration being spent, Emma crumpled into her chair, her momentarily defiant stand now replaced with abject forlornness. "I'm sorry," was all she could muster, as she bowed her head and wiped tears from her cheeks.

A heavy silence filled the room as the two women, one sitting, one standing, remained in frozen attitudes. Then Virginia spoke. "Here's what you could do, Emma: get a nice Get Well card and have all the students in your class sign it, and they can write little cheery messages. You can add your own—but nothing too personal. I'll drop it in the mail box in the Day Room. All mail is inspected.

Virginia paused, gazing down at Emma's bowed head and drooping shoulders. "I'm sorry, Emma, but that's about the only way you can legitimately communicate with Mercy."

Emma recognized that Virginia was trying to be helpful, but she still struggled with the realization that this meager expression of solicitude was all that was presently available to her. All the trite, worn expressions that were written endlessly and self-consciously on cards by people of all classes in expressing sympathy for the misfortunes of another human being—get well soon, we miss you, hurry back to us, god bless you, we're praying for you, keep your spirits up, you can lick this, we're all pulling for you—just seemed so paltry, so inadequate to sustain a woman of Mercy's sensitivities, as, alone, she faced the greatest challenge of her life: the certainty and acceptance of imminent death.

Lost in her thoughts, Emma now heard Virginia's voice again. "I have to go to a meeting, but why don't you stay here for a while until you're feeling calmer."

Emma glanced at her watch—a cheap Timex she had bought to replace the good watch she usually wore outside of prison because of the superintendent's warning against wearing any expensive jewelry—and said automatically, "I have to get to class." She left Virginia's office, walking like an automaton, lost in her tumultuous thoughts about Mercy. *There must be some other way I can communicate with her. There has to be! I'll find a way, no matter what the rules say!*

She headed toward her classroom, knowing that all the students would besiege her with questions about Mercy. She couldn't tell them just now. She couldn't bear to hear the shock and surprise and sorrow, feigned or felt, that would fill the air and demand to be professed and examined and indulgently extended. She resolved to say nothing today and tell them on Thursday at the end of the class, and then escape for the weekend.

She felt light-headed as she entered the classroom where Mercy's presence was keenly felt and Mercy's spirit was sharply etched. She ached for Mercy's smile and voice and gesture as she gathered and sorted workbooks for today's lesson. There would be no writing today; the time would be filled with busy, mechanical activities requiring no sharing, no possible opening of emotional spigots she wanted to keep tightly closed for the moment.

The students arrived and, as she had anticipated, already knew about Mercy's being in the medical unit and immediately bombarded her with questions about Mercy's condition. To all of their insistent inquiries, their teacher, unsmiling and unusually subdued, gave only one answer: she had heard nothing yet. Their disappointment was clearly evident, and a quietly sullen mood descended on the classroom. The time dragged to a point that it seemed like it was marching backwards whenever Emma glanced at her Timex. It took days for the class to end, and everyone dispensed with the usual pleasantries as they left the classroom.

30

On Thursday, twenty minutes before the end of the class, Emma collected all the workbooks. The students could sense from Emma's serious demeanor that something different was about to happen, and the air was charged with a crackling tension. Emma began speaking slowly.

"I've got some news about Mercy and I'm sorry to say it isn't good,"

Strong responses from students as they shifted in their seats, a few slamming their fists against their desks, others releasing strange sounds of anger and pity. Mary Louise, the only white student in the class besides the sarcastic Helen and known for her lady-like behavior, shouted "Shit!"

Emma raised her hand to quiet the group before continuing. "The cancer has spread from her breast to the bone marrow."

More sighs, shouts and exclamations from her audience.

"That's very bad," Inez said softly, and others shook their heads.

"Yes, I'm afraid it is," Emma said with a slight tremor in her voice, and the women could see that she was struggling to remain calm. Emma held up an oversized Get Well card decorated with small stars and hearts in vivid colors, as if the recipient had a mild case of the flu. "I thought we could all write a brief message and sign the card, to let her know we care and we're rooting for her,"

Emma said with a wan smile and little conviction in her voice. Everyone eagerly agreed.

Emma passed the card around and each woman wrote a sentence or two in pencil, enlisting Emma's help with "How do you spell...?" When everyone had finished, Emma put the card in its envelope but didn't seal it. She wanted to write her message to Mercy without the students' seeing it.

`"Will you deliver this to her?" Mariela asked.

"No, that's not permitted," Emma said evenly, trying to conceal her anger.

"The bastards!" exclaimed Mary Louise, once again out of character, but Emma could see that the students were clearly agitated at what they saw as the injustice of such harsh rules.

"You should ask the superintendent," Mariela suggested, and several women joined in a chorus of "Yeah!"

Emma remembered Virginia Ryan's warnings about any indication Emma might give of a special bond between Mercy and herself as possible—no, probable—cause for dismissal. "We'll see," was her noncommittal response.

Just then the guard opened the classroom door and pointed to her watch indicating it was time to leave. That broke the mounting tension in the room and Emma was grateful for the silence that surrounded her as she sat at her desk and now wrote her own message to Mercy. Mindful that in order for the card to get to Mercy, it had to be mailed from inside the prison where it would be opened and read, Emma knew she must be circumspect in what she said. Yet, she wanted to express her deep concern and show her personal support for Mercy.

Dear Mercy,

The entire class misses you and sends their

124

best wishes to you, as you can see from what they've
written. My thoughts and prayers are with you.
You are a great asset to our class and to me. Thank
you for all your help and we are all rooting for you.

Then she hesitated, her pen poised in mid-air, before muttering a defiant "Damn it" and writing,

I wish I could deliver these good wishes in person.
Emma

Let the authorities make of that what they wished. She'd deny any *bond* and say it was simply a basic charitable desire toward a dying woman.

She read her words again, regretting the stale use of the old clichés but recognizing that she couldn't possibly express her true feelings. Angrily, she sealed the envelope, addressed it to Mercy in the medical unit and dropped it in the mail shoot on her way out of the administration building.

Knowing Mercy was smart enough to read between the lines, Emma hoped that her real message of respect and fondness and gratitude would be received. As the main prison gate closed behind her, the air suddenly smelled fresher, and Emma greedily sucked it in with greedy, gulping sounds.

31

"Oliver, would you mind very much if we didn't go to the dinner dance at the club tonight?" Emma asked casually, when Oliver returned early from his office on Friday afternoon.

Emma had been reading in the sun-splashed sitting room off their master bedroom, trying to keep from thinking about Mercy, when Oliver came in, bent over and gave her his customary kiss on her cheek before heading into their bedroom to change his clothes. She carefully watched her husband's face for signs of annoyance or disappointment but all she saw was a look of mild surprise.

"Why?" was all he said from the other room in a neutral tone, and she could hear his loafers landing on the closet floor as he kicked them off.

"I'm just not feeling up to it," she replied.

"Are you okay, Em?" he asked, with a slight note of concern slipping into his voice.

"I'm fine," she said, but the weariness behind her words betrayed her. "It's just been a rough week."

"Where are the kids?"

"They took the dogs for a walk along the lake."

Oliver returned to the sitting room dressed in a sweat suit and sneakers. "I'm going for a run," he said. "Feel like joining me?"

For years they had kept up a regimen of three-mile runs together at least three times a week, but as Oliver saw forty advancing over the horizon, he had suddenly felt a need to double his exercise routine and now ran every day, except Sunday, either in the early morning or late afternoon.

"No, thanks," she said, throwing him an indulgent smile.

"Okay," he said cheerfully, turning toward their bedroom door. He took a few steps, turned, came back to the sofa where she was sitting and sat down next to her.

"What's bothering you, Em?" he asked softly and she was touched by his solicitude.

From the time that they had formed their agreement about her not showing a preoccupation with her prison work in their home, she had kept everything connected with her work to herself. But just now, with Oliver sitting beside her and asking so gently what was clearly troubling her, she felt that she could bend the rule and unburden herself of all the complicated and disturbing emotions she was feeling about Mercy.

She started to talk, first about what a strong, compassionate, intelligent and considerate woman she had discovered Mercy to be; then about the diagnosis and the death blow; and finally about the prison's obstacles to any expression of humanity and the haunting thought of Mercy's suffering and dying alone.

Her voice rose higher in pitch and the words rushed out in a rapidly building tempo as she shared her anguish and frustration. She was so caught up in her confessional monologue that she was not observing Oliver's reactions until she reached her conclusion, saying "She's in that medical unit, surrounded by strangers, and there's nothing I can do for her." Weary from her emotional outpouring, she finished speaking and, in a natural gesture, rested her head against her husband's shoulder, finding comfort in his strong, physical presence. Several seconds passed before she realized that he had said nothing, nor had he made any small return gesture—putting his arm around her or squeezing her shoulder – to comfort or reassure her of his understanding and support. His silence and perfect stillness grew ominous. Finally he spoke.

"You really have become quite the little crusader!"

Emma was startled at the sarcasm underlying his words, and she instantly pulled her head away from his shoulder and looked directly at him. After all the years they had been together, she could tell by the straight-line set of his lips and the clenched jaw that she had not misinterpreted his tone. He returned her stare, his puckered eyebrows crouching low above his piercing blue eyes.

"What's that supposed to mean?" she asked defensively.

"Just what I said," he replied, his stern visage never changing. "You're letting these prisoners take over your life. First it was this student or that student; now it's Mercy. I thought we had an agreement, Emma."

She was staring at his lips as they formed the words she couldn't quite believe she was hearing. This unexpected confrontation left her completely off-balance, and she struggled with a response.

"I don't recall breaking our agreement," she said weakly.

"What did you just finish telling me?" he asked angrily, rising from the sofa and standing in front of her.

"But you asked me what was the matter and I told you," she said, looking up at him and gesturing like a supplicant.

"Yes, you told me! You told me all about this Mercy person..."—she winced as she thought how close *this Mercy person* was to *those people*—"and how you wish you could help and comfort her. And that's why you're not up to going to the club tonight because you're emotionally drained from worrying about Mercy."

His voice was filled with petulance, she thought, like a little boy who didn't get what he wanted for Christmas. She looked away from him as his words cascaded down on her.

"This was not part of our deal, Emma. Maybe you haven't spoken about your prison work until now, but it's clear to me that you're totally preoccupied with those people."

My god, he said it! Her brain screamed—he actually said *those people*. She reacted as though he had hit her, sinking deeper into the sofa in a defensive crouch against another blow as his angry words continued to shower down on her.

"What was supposed to be a few-hours-a-week volunteer job has taken over your life, and taken you away from your first responsibility, your family. No matter what you're doing with me or the kids, you always seem distracted, your mind forever somewhere else, and I know what you're thinking about, Emma: your students and now Mercy."

"That's not true," she said feebly, suddenly feeling totally vulnerable and very, very tired.

"Look at what happened last Christmas," he said, eager to prove his point. "You were so busy running around to all the local churches coordinating the toy drive for the prisoners' children that you barely had time to celebrate the holiday with your own children and me. Then you started that Christmas card collection drive, asking all our friends and neighbors to donate boxes of cards that might be left over from last year, but you knew they would buy new boxes to give you, and Michelle Heredy and Carol Mumford both gave you big checks for cards and gifts. It's embarrassing to me. And even on Christmas morning, you had us all helping you collect the last-minute donated gifts and deliver them to the prison when we should have been home, following our traditions and unwrapping our own presents. And then Christmas dinner was late and…"

She interrupted him. "You and the kids offered to help me. I didn't ask you."

"We offered to help so that we could have our own Christmas, once you finished seeing that everybody else had a good one. You're playing lady bountiful and putting everyone ahead of your family and I've had enough." His voice was rising in anger and then he stopped, as though struggling to gain control of his indignation. "I'm going to the club with or without you," was his final declaration in a lower voice, and he moved into their bedroom, leaving her on the sofa feeling rejected and lonely.

32

Oliver's harsh words rang in her ears as she sat motionless on the sofa, unable to move, replaying his seemingly endless series of accusations. Finally, she let them drift over her head as her thoughts turned inward and she reflected on the previous Christmas which had been, she had to admit, an unexpectedly hectic holiday for her.

Virginia Ryan had casually asked her if she could spend some extra time helping with the Christmas toy drive. Before agreeing, she had discussed it with Mercy.

"Christmas is really the happiest time of the year for a lot of the ladies, especially those mothers with children," Mercy told Emma with shining eyes and that wide, dazzling smile. "People are so kind and generous at that time of year, it really lifts your spirits to know they care.

Having heard Mercy's ringing endorsement, Emma couldn't say no. Virginia Ryan explained how the toy drive worked.

"We make a lot of paper stars and distribute them to the inmates with children under sixteen. They then ask their kids what they'd like for Christmas, and you'd be surprised how reasonable their requests are. Most often it's a doll for the younger girls and some clothing for the older ones. For the boys it's some piece of athletic equipment or toys connected with war and maybe a video game. It's seldom some big item like a bicycle or a puppy. You can tell that life has already taught these kids to have modest expectations, and the mothers understand that everything is donated, so they can guide their kids. Anyway, each child can ask for three things that the mother writes on a star and all the stars are distributed to all the churches in the vicinity.

The churches put up a Christmas tree right after Thanksgiving, decorated only with the stars. The members of the church can read what's on each star and then choose a star and buy the gifts listed. They're supposed to return them to their church no later than one week before Christmas, and that's when we need all the help we can get, in driving around to all the churches and picking up the presents."

"We have a big SUV to accommodate the five of us and our two dogs," Emma commented.

"Just the type of vehicle we need," Virginia said, smiling. "You'd be surprised how many toys and clothes and games are collected. And, of course, some people will always run past the deadline in buying the gifts and getting them back to the church. Some people bring in the gifts wrapped and since everything coming into the prison has to be inspected, those gifts have to be unwrapped, so there's always a lot of work right up to Christmas day, but it really represents the true spirit of Christmas and everyone feels good about it."

Virginia stopped to answer her phone and spoke briefly before returning to the topic with Emma.

"I have to admit, we cheat a little," she said with a sly grin. "We go through the stars when the inmates return them to us and we give the stars with the most expensive requests to the Episcopalians, but, bless their hearts, they always come through."

"That's my church," Emma said brightly, then realized that during the busy month of December she and Oliver had only attended services on Christmas day and had not known about the stars program. "I'll be glad to help," she said quickly, hoping to make amends for a rush of guilt.

True to Virginia's description, the weeks and days leading up to Christmas were busy ones for Emma who entered wholeheartedly into this worthy project. She delivered stars to various churches and collected the packages at night, after dinner with her family was finished and everyone had retreated to a private space.

Never had she felt the Christmas spirit more keenly or deeply. She enlisted Carol Mumford's help and this friend gladly joined Emma in making her nightly rounds to the churches and loading the SUV with the presents. They would put aside those that had been wrapped and return to Emma's house where they might spend another hour carefully unwrapping the gifts.

Emma remembered her happy childhood Christmas experiences, especially the excitement of unwrapping presents. She asked Virginia if wrapping paper and trimmings could be brought into the prison separately and then the mothers could wrap their children's donated gifts, adding a personal touch for the inmates.

Emma was disappointed when Virginia explained that ordinary scissors and even scotch tape with the serrated cutting edge on the dispenser would never be allowed in the prison, as they could be used as weapons. Even a simple pleasure like opening presents is denied the children of inmates, Emma thought sadly, but then consoled herself with the thought that at least the kids were getting gifts, which was something to look forward to, when they visited their mothers at Christmas.

With the checks that Michele Heredy and Carol had given Emma, she bought extra presents for unexpected holiday visits by children.

"This is one charitable cause where I can see exactly how my money is being spent," Carol quipped.

Oliver would occasionally wander past the guest room, observing Emma and Carol chatting and laughing while removing the wrappings from some of the gifts. He would smile indulgently—condescendingly, Emma thought—and quickly move on. Emma never asked him to help and he never offered.

One night, shortly after their wrapping ritual had started, when Oliver appeared at the door, Carol said, "Why don't you get your butt in here and give us a hand?" in her usual direct, wisecracking manner.

"No thanks," Oliver said, returning her smile, "I've got work to do so my wife can indulge in her charities." The sarcastic undertone beneath the bantering humor was obvious.

"Okay, Scrooge," Carol shouted at Oliver's retreating figure, but Emma said nothing, sensing Oliver's barely concealed disapproval, or, she wondered, was it resentment? The thought drifted away as Carol made some crack about a doll that looked like a hooker, and the two women laughed.

"I wonder what the inmates might want for Christmas...besides freedom and a man!" Carol said. Carol's thoughts never strayed too far from sex, a subject she talked candidly and frequently about. "I can't imagine going for years without a good old-fashioned tumble in the hay. That must be the hardest part of being in prison: no men! That and being separated from your children."

Emma decided not to tell Carol what she had learned about the sexual outlets that women in prison found.

33

When Emma next visited Virginia Ryan's office, she had asked, "Do the inmates get any gifts?"

"Only if they have families who care enough to bring them something or send them a present," Virginia said. "And you'd be amazed how many presents contain hidden contraband—drugs, cell phones, even weapons. We go nuts around here trying to check each package thoroughly at this time of year." Emma nodded, recognizing that for the prisoners and their families on the outside, there was a constant battle between them and the authorities.

"What the women miss most, I think," Virginia continued, "is being able to send Christmas cards to their loved ones."

"They're not able to send cards?" Emma repeated, surprised by this revelation that she had never thought about.

"Not unless they're donated," Virginia said, "and we never get enough to go around and then there's the cost of postage."

This brief exchange planted the seed in Emma's mind to address this need. That night at home, she sat at a desk in the family room and composed a brief letter.

> *Dear Friends,*
> *As many of you know, I've been volunteering at the*
> *Ashroken Women's Correctional Facility—a fancy*

label for prison. I make no judgment on the quality of justice that the inmates have received, or on their guilt or innocence. I only know that at this time of the year, the separation from loved ones is keenly felt by the women, who can't even send a holiday greeting card to their families. This is where you could help. If you have holiday cards left over from previous years, would you consider donating them and brightening someone else's holidays immeasurably? Or perhaps, when you're out doing your holiday shopping, you might come upon an inexpensive package of cards that you would be willing to donate. Whether it's one card or a box, anything you care to give would be greatly appreciated. Just drop them off at my house and I'll see that they're all delivered. It really would make a great difference.

Bless you.

She signed it, "*Emma*," and sent the note to over seventy-five families including neighbors, families they knew from the club or people who were former clients of Oliver's.

The response, whether from genuine concern or from embarrassment at not replying—Emma didn't care—had been huge. Boxes of cards stacked to the ceiling soon filled a corner of the guest room. Michelle Heredy had appeared in Emma's driveway one afternoon and Emma, who had gone out to meet her, saw that the back seat of Michelle's Mercedes sedan was filled with boxes of cards. Michelle had also handed Emma another large check "for anything else you need for the prisoners to give them a little Christmas cheer," she said, and Emma, genuinely touched with this brassy, good-hearted woman's instinctive generosity, embraced Michelle warmly.

Emma and Carol had loaded Emma's SUV with all the cards, leaving just enough room for the two women in the front seat, and delivered them to the prison where it took hours for the guards to inspect each box of cards.

Virginia Ryan was very pleased. "You've really outdone yourself, Emma," she said after all the cards had been delivered to her office, with stacks of them spilling out into the corridor. "With this many cards, we can distribute four or five to every inmate. Congratulations."

"And here's a large donation from one generous friend which I thought could cover postage," Emma said, handing Michelle's check, made out to cash, to Virginia.

Virginia looked at the check, puckered her lips and let out a low whistle. "A very generous friend! This is terrific, Emma."

Emma always felt like a young girl getting praise from a teacher when Virginia complimented her on anything.

"My friends and neighbors really came through for me," she said, beaming.

"If you'll give me their names and addresses, I'll send an official Thank You note," Virginia said.

"I'll have to go through my address book and give you a list after the first of the year," Emma said, thoroughly pleased with how she had started and successfully completed this project. She had not given any thought to how all the time spent in doing this work might affect her family. Now her husband was clearly unhappy and their relationship was faced with new challenges.

34

When Oliver returned from the dinner-dance at the club, Emma was reading in the family room. She heard him come in and go directly upstairs. Then she heard his footsteps coming down the stairs. She looked up from her book when he entered the family room, looking slightly disheveled. A quick glance told her that he had been drinking—not enough to make him drunk but enough to exceed the driving limit.

He walked to within a few feet of her chair and stopped, but did not sit down.

"There's no greater fun than going to a dinner-dance alone," he said, and the uneven shifting of his voice confirmed his condition. "Everyone wanted to know where you were, and I told them that you were a little under the weather. I couldn't tell them that you were weary from worrying about inmates at the prison."

She had forced herself to read a book to get her mind off of their heated exchanges earlier that evening and to calm down. She was unprepared to start another caustic exchange, and she made no reply.

"We can't go on like this, Emma," he said. "I want my wife back!"

He turned away from her and started walking toward the stairs, still talking. "I want my life as it was before you got involved in this ridiculous mission of yours." He disappeared up the stairs.

She sat silently, not reading, the book still opened but resting on her lap, reflecting on what had just happened. Oliver was clearly giving her an ultimatum: give up your volunteer work or else. Or else what? Separation? Divorce? He wanted his wife back, he said. What he really wanted, she thought with mounting indignation, was for her to have no other role than his wife, no separate identity except as an appendage to the successful, admired architect. In the twenty-first century did Oliver really feel this way? Then she realized that she had, until recently, been content to be an appendage, first to her brilliant, egocentric parents and, next, to her husband.

For how many years had she been content with the reflected glory she enjoyed as the wife of a dynamic, successful man, and with her ancillary role as bedmate, companion and mother of his children? She recognized how, over the nearly fifteen years of their marriage, her subordinate role was so set, so satisfactory to Oliver that he thought of her, justifiably, as being content with the part she played, and now could not conceive of her desire to expand her world beyond the confines of family, friends and his clients. He was happy and content; why shouldn't she be, too?

She rested her head against the back of the wingback chair, her mind racing. She knew that they were at a crossroads. If she pulled back, gave up her volunteer work at the prison, focused exclusively on her family and restricted her volunteer work to her children's schools, everything would be fine again. She would gaily chatter away at the country club, at luncheons, dinner parties and fund-raising events, secure in her attractiveness, her poise, her ability to charm her husband's clients.

She saw herself performing these repetitious, boring tasks in an endless projection of years, a tiresome attenuation of superficial posturing, a sacrifice of herself for the good of her husband's business and his image of the dutiful wife.

She thought of the young, idealistic man she fell in love with at college, who had wanted success, and, coming from his humble, impoverished background, who could blame him? But he had also dreamed of using his talents in designing good homes for the poor. Then he had complacently succumbed to catering to a newly moneyed class, enjoying their admiring and financially rewarding responses to the glossy houses he designed for them. He seemed oblivious, or totally indifferent, to their closed-ranks attitude to the rest of the world. In this restricted environment he seemed content, while she was finding it increasingly hard to breathe.

Her thoughts turned to Mercy and her students, and the indefinable ways they had opened her eyes to such a vast scope of life beyond anything she had ever experienced and, in so doing, had aroused her compassion and desire to play an active part in helping or changing or improving—doing something, anything—to touch the lives of others.

She had discovered that such actions on behalf of others enriched and expanded her own life, and she also knew that having started down this course, she would not give it up. She would be her own person, and Oliver would have to accept this. Then she thought of his parting words and shuddered at the conflict to come. She didn't want to lose her husband or break up her family. But she couldn't sacrifice her identity or her growth to the preservation of her marriage either.

35

Emma turned off the downstairs lights and went up to their bedroom. The lights were off and Oliver seemed to be asleep. She moved into her walk-in closet, closed the door and quietly undressed. She slipped quickly into bed and lay on her side away from her husband. In the silent darkness, she listened to Oliver's quick, shallow breathing, signaling that he was only pretending to sleep. Engulfed in silence, all her senses alert, her body rigid with anxiety, Emma hoped that he would not continue their confrontation tonight. But he said nothing and she felt the air crackling with tension as they both lay in the same bed, facing opposite sides, neither capable of breaching the great wall that currently divided them.

Mercy's face floated before her half-closed lids and Emma was again consumed with concern. She pictured Mercy in her prison hospital bed, the light that had always danced in her eyes now dimmed from pain or drugs, replaced by fear of facing death alone.

Emma had seen on television the starving poor of India, the horrendous genocidal waves that swept across African countries and the pitiful plight of the homeless right here in America. She always responded by being momentarily sympathetic to all the deprivation and suffering but then Marta would announce that dinner was ready or one of the children would ask her a question, or the phone would ring and any distraction was all it took to put her in another mindset and forget about the problems of humanity. Anyway, they were all so immense that she could never decide what to do, except maybe send a small check to ameliorate a particular condition.

Now there was Mercy, who was not a stranger, who did not represent great masses of people in some distant, abstracted way and who had touched Emma's life at deeply emotional points. She felt that she was Mercy's lifeline, the only one who could reach out to her at the hardest, scariest moment of anyone's life: the imminence of death. She felt a connection to Mercy as strong as if she were a member of her family. She could not abandon another human being who needed her. Such an act of betrayal and indifference would diminish herself as a person.

A defiant resolve welled up inside Emma. For whatever reasons, Mercy, and, yes, her students too, had become vitally linked to Emma's sense of self-worth. She would do everything she could to help Mercy and she would continue her volunteer work at the prison. This was non-negotiable, regardless of the consequences to her marriage. If Oliver could not accept her on these terms, then it was he who would initiate the rupture. And she would bend or go around any prison rule that kept her from offering support to Mercy.

Feeling that she had made a momentous personal decision, Emma closed her eyes and soon drifted off to sleep.

PART FOUR

36

The next several days were awkward ones of silent truce in the Granby household, as Emma and Oliver performed their daily routines and managed to keep a civilly wide distance between each other, exchanging only necessary words involving the children or schedules or household demands.

Emma made no mention of her work to anyone except Carol Mumford, but even with Carol she shared nothing about her current problems with Oliver. She went off to the prison on the following Tuesday and Thursday, feeling Mercy's absence from the classroom intensely.

Emma had been forming a plan that she now put into effect. She called June Sperry, the garrulous volunteer in the medical unit who had originally recommended that Emma try volunteer work at the prison. Emma invited June for lunch as a restaurant in the city and June, surprised by the invitation from someone she hardly knew, accepted eagerly.

Emma recalled her early contact with June when Emma had called her to inquire about possible areas in the prison needing volunteers. In her enthusiastic voice, June had encouraged Emma to see if she liked working in a prison, cautioning her that it wasn't for everyone—a fact that Virginia Ryan had also emphasized when Emma first appeared for an interview.

"This is a harsh environment and the women are tough," Virginia had explained. "Some of them come in here already hardened, and some of the younger ones, the first-time offenders, get a college education in crime before they leave. Over sixty percent of our volunteers don't last more than six months and many leave after only a week or two." Virginia paused before adding, "This isn't a happy place to work in. Sometimes I think it almost takes a special vocation, like missionary work."

Virginia had seen Emma's worried look and added in a lighter tone, "But it can be very rewarding if you can find your niche. We have volunteers who have been here for decades. One volunteer, Mary Welch, has been working in our nursery for twenty-seven years. The inmates love her. She's raised her own kids and teaches the women how to take proper care of their babies—basic skills most of them don't possess. I call her Saint Mary."

Emma recalled those cautionary exchanges as she waited for June at the restaurant and formed a mental picture of how June might look, based solely on her voice, filled with infectious enthusiasm. Since June was a friend of Carol Mumford's mother, Emma assumed that she would be in her sixties and was surprised to see a small, thin woman appearing to be only in her early fifties approaching the table with a big smile and an extended hand.

"Emma?" said the voice that was instantly identifiable as June's. Emma rose and the two women greeted each other with the warmth of sisters-in-battle. Pleasantries were exchanged, the menu inspected and selections given to the waiter who shortly delivered glasses of chardonnay for the two women.

June's pretty, open face matched her ebullient personality and conversation about their prison experiences flowed easily. Emma learned that June was a neighbor of Carol Mumford's mother, which accounted for the age discrepancy. After lunch, over coffee, Emma broached the topic for which this meeting had been planned.

"Have you ever grown fond of a particular inmate in the hospital?" Emma asked, trying to sound casual.

"Oh, my goodness, yes," June quickly responded. "It's hard not to. Some of the patients who are seriously ill feel so vulnerable and their nice side comes out and you can't help but feel sorry for them and give them some extra attention. We're all human, after all, and it's the only kind thing you can do for them"

Emma was delighted to hear June's compassionate response and decided to be direct with her, after one more test.

"So you bend the rule about not forming any bond with the prisoners or showing favoritism?" Emma said in a conspiratorial stage whisper, leaning towards June.

June laughed and reached for Emma's hand. "Oh God, yes, all the time! But that's our little secret."

"And you've never gotten into trouble?" Emma asked in a teasing tone.

Still laughing, June replied, "No, never. But everyone isn't watched as closely in the prison hospital as they are in the rest of the prison, so I have more independence..." June paused, smiled and winked at Emma. "And opportunity to bend the rules."

Both women took sips of their coffee.

"June, have you seen Mercy Campbell, a new patient?"

June's eyes widened. "Yes, she's a delight! A very sad case. Incurable cancer."

"Mercy was my classroom aide in my GED program," Emma said, looking directly at June. "She's a wonderful woman and I've grown very fond of her, I admit."

June smiled and nodded in agreement, encouraging Emma to continue. "As you know, she hasn't got very long to live, and her only relatives are two daughters and neither of them will probably visit her. I don't want her to feel she's all alone."

The sad expression that quickly enveloped June's face reassured Emma that she was gaining an ally. Emma reached over and squeezed June's hand.

"Would you be willing to deliver a message to her from me? I know it's a violation of the rules and you and I could both be dismissed if we got caught, and if you think it's too risky and don't want to do it, I'll certainly understand," Emma said quickly.

June laid her hand on Emma's and without hesitation said, "Of course I will."

Emma laughed with nervous relief. After Emma had paid the check, the two women, confirmed in their new conspiratorial bond, left the restaurant arm in arm.

37

That very evening after dinner, when Oliver had gone off to some civic meeting and the children were watching television in the family room, Emma retreated to her bedroom and composed her letter to Mercy.

Dear Mercy,

I am so sorry that I cannot come to visit you but my friend has agreed to deliver this note to you.

Mercy, I cannot thank you enough for all the help you've given me and for showing me how to be a more effective teacher. You've opened my eyes to so much suffering and injustice in the world and you've helped me to be a more sympathetic and understanding person. All the students miss you but I miss you more, for you have become my valued friend.

I know this is a very challenging time for you but please know that I am with you in spirit and my prayers and thoughts are flying your way.

Your friend,

Emma

Emma delivered her hand-written note to June in the prison parking lot. The next day at home, Emma got a call from June.

"Oh, Emma, she was thrilled to get your note," June said with genuine excitement. She read it quickly and gave it back to me for fear that someone would find it when changing her bed or examining her. She asked me to thank you and to tell you she's so proud to know you think of her as a friend. She thinks you're a wonderful teacher and she sends you her love."

Emma felt a wave of joy and sadness sweeping over her as June's words came rushing out of the phone. Then she had another idea.

"June, do you think I could send Mercy some flowers?"

There was a momentary silence at the other end before June, who had been considering Emma's question, replied.

"They couldn't come from you, Emma, but I bring in flowers from my garden for the hospital ward and nobody's ever made a fuss. My lilac bushes are blooming right now and I'll bring in a big bouquet and place it near Mercy's bed and secretly let her know they're from you to her. How's that?"

"You're terrific!" Emma exclaimed. Her fondness for June, as well as appreciation for her cleverness, was growing daily.

38

A few days later, June called with more news. The excitement in her voice was contagious as her words tumbled out.

"The prison notified Mercy's daughter, Hope, of her mother's illness. They sent the notice to the California rehabilitation center, which was the only address they had for her, but the center had a forwarding address and she's coming to see her mother. Emma, she's coming!"

Emma heard the news with her own sense of growing excitement, mingled with relief. Mercy would not die alone. If only Charity, the other daughter, could be reunited with her mother, Emma thought, after she ended the phone conversation.

Emma could understand how Charity could cut her mother out of her life after Mercy had killed Charity's boyfriend. Mercy had never shared any details of this event and Emma had never dared to ask any questions. But surely, Emma speculated, given the current circumstances, Charity would want to reconcile with her mother. When Hope arrived, she would speak to her.

Emma was now writing notes regularly to Mercy, telling her about the class and news of individual students. With no hesitation and even eagerness, June would find a time to slip Emma's notes to Mercy. Mercy would read them and return them to June, whispering her response, which June would then relay to Emma via phone.

The lilac flowers from June's garden had been especially prized by Mercy when June whispered that they were from Emma. In gratitude, the next time she went to the main street of Claremont Heights, Emma ordered a large floral bouquet to be delivered to June's house. The two women were now solidly bonded in their humanitarian cause, and Emma was amazed how eagerly and inventively June Sperry had entered into their conspiracy.

39

Virginia Ryan had found another aide for Emma's classroom. Her name was Stella. When she appeared at the door of Emma's classroom with Virginia, Emma was startled to see a small, thin figure, looking no more than late teens, with long straight hair and a beautifully shaped face, delicate features and deep-set dark gray eyes.

"Stella's a high school graduate and had a year of community college," Virginia explained.

Stella was sweet and pliant and did everything willingly that Emma asked her to do, but she showed no initiative, was very shy with the students and seemed intimidated by everyone. In turn, the students mostly ignored her. Emma noted the marked contrast between Stella and Mercy and came to appreciate her former aide more.

In the preparation time before class when Emma and Stella were alone, Emma learned Stella's story. Despite her youthful, almost childlike appearance, Stella was twenty-four and had already been in prison for three years. Her story was another one of betrayed trust.

Stella's boyfriend, who worked as a motel clerk and was a compulsive gambler, had given her some expensive jewelry for Christmas and her birthday, claiming he had bought it with gambling winnings. Then he was arrested for a string of house burglaries and all the jewelry was identified as coming from the burglarized houses. Stella was tried as an accessory and given a stiff sentence of six to eight years. She swore she knew nothing about her boyfriend's criminal life but the jury didn't believe her.

Emma remembered Mercy's warning that most of the prisoners claimed to be innocent and they always tried to "get over" you—convince you—of their innocence. Yet there was such a naive and unaffected sweetness about Stella that Emma could see how easily she could be duped.

What troubled Emma, as she reflected on her students' versions of their reasons for being sent to prison, was the possibility that their accounts could be true, and if they were, then terrible injustices had been committed against them. In many cases the ready availability of drugs to escape the grim life in the ghetto or the barrio had hooked girls as young as twelve or thirteen, following the path of parents or older siblings and leading inevitably to prostitution or petty crimes, some of which unexpectedly turned violent. Then they found themselves locked away for a significant portion of their lives, only to return again to the same neighborhood, the same friends, the same influences that had led them to trouble in the first place.

This cycle seemed endless and few could escape it. Most of the prisoners were never rehabilitated. Scrubbing floors and cleaning toilets and working in the laundry or the cafeteria offered few new horizons. The prison beauty shop did offer a limited number of women a chance to learn a skill that could profitably be applied when they were released from prison. But Emma saw how their low self-esteem, the habitual subjugation of their spirit by callous and sometimes sadistic guards, and the seething inferno of nearly a thousand women locked together in cramped cells and forced to obey rules and orders from sun-up to sundown, offered little chance of hope for a different or better life.

Her students, at least, she reminded herself, still had a spark of hope left, as demonstrated by their desire to get their high school equivalency diploma. She had a special group and she had to fan that flame of desire for change and renewal. Still, she thought, the odds are so stacked against them for any kind of decent life; it requires heroic strength and determination to break the pattern. She recognized that she could be an instrument of redemption. She had found a calling that challenged and thrilled her, as nothing had before.

Emma thought of the personal histories that the women had shared with the class through their writing. Chantelle was a fiercely proud African-American woman, about Emma's age, whose husband had become a crack addict after losing his job and not being able to find another. To support his habit, he became a dealer and when the police raided the apartment that he and Chantelle shared with their two-year-old twin boys, they found a large stash of crack and arrested Chantelle along with her husband.

Although her husband testified that she had nothing to do with his drug dealing and had no knowledge of it, the jury didn't like her proud manner and aggressive defiance and found her guilty as an accessory.

Then there was Lucy, the shy African-American student who found self-confidence after winning the class spelling trophy. Her mother and aunt had been selling drugs from the apartment they shared with Lucy, and when neighbors complained of all the seedy characters going in and out of the apartment at all hours of the day and night, the police raided it and found drugs. Lucy's mother and aunt swore that Lucy was the pusher and because they were both elderly, they were believed and Lucy, strongly protesting her innocence, was sent to prison.

Emma could not conceive of that kind of betrayal by a mother against her daughter, but she tended to believe Lucy's story because she saw that Lucy was endlessly struggling, through her writing, with this betrayal.

The saddest case of all, Emma thought, was Anita, who had emigrated illegally from El Salvador at sixteen to join her older brother in America. She worked cleaning houses and met a young man who professed love, got her pregnant and then vanished. Anita had the baby and was forced to leave it alone for three-to-four-hour stretches while she went out to clean houses.

The brother complained that the baby was always crying. Anita returned home from a cleaning job one day and found the baby dead in its crib. Fear gripped her and she wrapped the baby in several blankets and hid the body in a chest at the foot of her bed. Her brother never asked where the baby was and Anita kept her secret until the stench rising from the chest was unbearable. One day she returned to the apartment she shared with her brother and found police waiting for her. Her brother had turned her in.

An autopsy showed the baby had died from suffocation, and because she had hidden the body, Anita was accused of smothering her baby. Frightened and confused by all the legal procedures she was subjected to, she became practically a mute, and her public defender submitted a plea of guilty with mitigating circumstances. Anita received an eight-to twelve-year sentence. Her brother never visited her.

Mariela was a different case, but equally sad. This very bright girl had been sexually abused by her uncle from the time she was seven. At eleven she had told her mother what had been happening for years, but her mother refused to believe her. Mariela's father was an alcoholic who, when drinking, would beat Mariela, her mother and her two younger sisters. Mariela escaped from this family hell at fifteen when she ran away with a twenty-three-year-old man who promised to marry her but took her to another city and forced her into prostitution. He, too, would physically abuse her when she offered any objections to the endless johns she was forced to service each day.

One night, she picked up an older man in his sixties and took him to a motel. Rather than having sex, he said he just wanted to hold her. They got into bed without undressing and he put his arms around her and stroked her hair and kept saying, "Ruthie, Ruthie." Soon he had fallen asleep. Mariela knew that she had to turn more tricks that night or be beaten by her pimp. She then decided that she would take the old man's wallet and leave the man in the motel room. In fumbling to get his wallet out of his pant's pocket, he woke up and gave her a hard shove.

Suddenly her brain exploded with hatred for all men and she got up and grabbed a knife that she carried in her bag for protection, and, as he was rising from the bed, she plunged it into his neck. He looked up at her with complete surprise turning to shock, but in that moment he was her father, her uncle, her pimp, and all the men who had used and debased her, and in an uncontrollable fury she stabbed him again and again.

He fell on the floor and lay in a widening pool of blood. Her next action was unfathomable, for she lay back down on the bed and cried hysterically until, exhausted, she fell asleep. Some hours later she was awakened by a loud knocking on the door, which she refused to answer. It turned out to be her pimp who, fearing that she had been hurt and he had lost a valuable property, had gotten the manager to open the door. When he saw the old man lying on the floor, he immediately vanished and the manager called the police.

Mariela admitted that she had killed the man but offered no explanation for why she did it. Her trial was speedy and the sentence severe: twenty years to life. She had been at Ashroken now for eleven years and during that entire time she was obsessed with her guilt. She wrote endlessly about the man she had killed and the information that had come out about him during her trial: that he had lost his wife recently, named Ruth; that he was described as a loving father and grandfather and a man who helped others.

Her creative mind dwelled on the sorrow he had felt in losing his life-time companion and why, in desperation, he had sought Mariela's company to soothe his loneliness. She speculated on the years he could have enjoyed if she had not deprived him of life. She would not, could not, forgive herself, and dwelt in a fathomless abyss of self-loathing and guilt, made more poignant by her sharp intellect, strong, unswerving conscience and insightful writings.

In reflecting on Mariela's history, Emma couldn't help but note that all the abuse this girl had taken from so many had ultimately condemned her to an intense self-loathing which she could not overcome, despite her obvious intellectual gifts.

Emma thought of all the advantages she had enjoyed in her life and wondered if she would have acted any differently if placed in her students' positions. Inevitably she knew the answer was probably not. Through her student's histories she had come to feel that life was just the luck of the draw, as they say, and with few, extraordinary exceptions, the pattern of one's life for the majority was usually set at birth: your parents, where you were born, your social and financial circumstances, family members, the cultural norms that influenced your future. Now she had come to believe that justice was neither blind nor impartial, and mercy was a quality that our society gave lip service to, but was missing from our legal system.

40

Stella had only been with Emma for a month when she didn't appear at the regular pre-class time. Shortly before class was scheduled to begin, Virginia Ryan came into the classroom.

"Emma, I'm sorry," Virginia said in a calm voice, "but I'm afraid I've got more bad news."

Emma immediately thought that the bad news involved Mercy and steeled herself for the worst.

"Stella was attacked last night by another inmate whose advances she rebuffed."

On hearing that the news was about Stella, Emma first felt relief, followed soon by concern for her new aide.

"How is she? Emma asked.

"She's got a broken nose and two missing front teeth and several bruised ribs and a black eye. More than anything, she's scared."

Emma instantly conjured up a scene with some woman twice the size of Stella administering such a ferocious beating, and the mere thought of such intense violence made her queasy.

"Emma, you're as white as a sheet," Virginia said with genuine concern filtering into her usually starched voice. "You'd better sit down."

Emma followed Virginia's suggestion but she still felt lightheaded. This prison world was so alien to anything she had ever experienced or even dreamed could exist. "How could one woman do that to another woman?" Emma asked in almost a wail.

Virginia, standing by her side, patted her shoulder and said, "The strong will always prey upon the weak, whether man or woman. It's the same on the outside world, only more oblique, more civilized. Here it's done at a primal level and is much more direct. That's the only difference."

Emma didn't want to accept Virginia's simple rule of the jungle as applying to most people in or out of prison, but she had a flashback to the brief time she had been involved in real estate and remembered how vicious the female agents were—all dressed so professionally with a polite, cultured veneer—in stealing her *For Sale* signs and undermining her creditability with potential customers in every way possible. In here, she thought, with the controlled environment and limited resources, physical violence was the equivalent of what the female realty agents had done to her.

Emma was getting an education in the nastier, most primitive side of her fellow females which distressed her, but she clung to her belief in goodness, too, conjuring up the concern that her students had displayed for each other and especially for Mercy. Of course, Mercy represented both goodness and, if the records were correct, a capacity for violence in one single act. This thought made Emma more confused and distressed.

Virginia's voice interrupted Emma's reflections. "I'm not sure I have anyone who could replace Stella right now."

"Don't bother. I can manage," Emma said, and she could see the relief on Virginia's face.

"Are you feeling well enough to have a class today?" Virginia asked solicitously, and Emma, welcoming the interactions with her students as a distraction from her dark thoughts, assured Virginia that she was fine.

41

Shortly after Virginia left, the students arrived and were full of news about Stella. Even though Emma didn't want to hear any more, she sensed that the students needed to vent, so, with a blank expression and only a half-tuned ear, she let them talk.

"It was Monica, that big butch dyke who was hot for Stella," Anita said.

"She's a bad one, that one," added Inez

"She kept followin' Stella around. I seen it all the time when we was in the Day Room," said Chantelle.

"And she was offering Stella little presents, like cigarettes and candy, and Stella kept refusing," Mary Louise added.

"And last night, after dinner," said Columbia, her face flushed with anger, "she grabbed Stella when she was comin' out of the bathroom and tried to kiss her. And Stella pushed her away and then Monica just went nuts and started beatin' on Stella somethin' fierce. And by the time the guards separated them, Stella was just lyin' in a heap on the floor, all doubled up and whimperin' like a baby."

"And," Inez said, eager to complete the story, "they carried Monica out, kickin' and cursin' and it took four guards to get that crazy bitch under control and haul her ass to the box."

Emma had to remind herself again that *the box* was prison slang for solitary confinement.

"She's one mean motherfucker, that one!" Inez shouted, and the class erupted in nervous giggles.

"They took Stella to the medical unit," Mariela said, and now no student could think of any other detail to add so they looked expectantly at Emma.

Try as she might not to allow all the vivid details that erupted from the students to infiltrate her already clouded brain, Emma now saw some of the more sordid images before her eyes, and again she felt lightheaded. Raising her hand to assure silence, she spoke in a strange, faraway voice.

"I'm sorry to hear this sad news. It's upsetting to all of us, isn't it?"

Most of the students shook their heads in agreement. "Would you like to send Stella a Get Well card, like the one we sent to Mercy?" Emma asked, barely thinking. More nods of agreement and a chorus of "Yeah."

With certainty Emma knew that neither she nor her students could focus on any work today, so she had them spend the time writing personal notes to Stella while she completed a makeshift design of a card.

By the end of the class Emma felt exhausted.

42

When Emma returned home from the prison that afternoon, she found Marta in the kitchen preparing dinner. The two boys were in the family room playing a video game, yelling and imitating sounds of death and destruction. Emma moved upstairs and found Susie in her room working on a science project for school.

"Need any help?" Emma casually inquired.

"No thanks, Mom," the ever independent Susie said.

"Where's Daddy?" Emma asked and Susie replied "He was home earlier but he went for a run."

Since there was over an hour before dinner and Emma had a splitting headache from all the events at the prison, she called down to Marta, saying that she was going to take a short nap and headed for the master bedroom. There she found her husband's dress slacks lying across the bed where he must have tossed them in changing clothes for his run. One of the few housewifely chores I do, she thought as she picked his pants off the bed and headed toward the closet with them.

When she came out of the walk-in closet, she spotted a folded piece of paper on the floor that she assumed must have fallen out of Oliver's pants.

She picked it up and casually glanced at the visible writing – a neat, flowery hand had written *Oliver* on the front of the folded paper. Then she halted in mid-step and looked more intently at the writing. It was unmistakably a woman's. Finally, she unfolded the paper and read the entire message. It was only two sentences.

Oliver, can we meet at our usual place this
afternoon? I've decided to leave Ken and
really need to talk. Karen

Emma, in a daze, walked over to the bed and sat at the edge, reading the note again. Her headache was now so intense that she thought the throbbing at her temples would burst through her skin. Her sight was blurry and there was a constant humming in her ears.

She knew immediately who Karen was. Karen Phelps was a lawyer in a firm whose offices were in the same building—on the same floor actually—as Oliver's office. Emma and Oliver had occasionally met Karen and Ken Phelps at social gatherings, and Emma recalled that she thought Karen was attractive, lively and a bit too flirtatious with other women's husbands. It all seemed rather innocent, though, and, besides, she never thought of Oliver as being the straying type. Well, obviously, she was wrong. Here was the damnable proof!

Again she read the note, although she could barely make out the words. Between Mercy and Stella and now this, she felt overwhelmed and helpless. The ringing in her ears grew louder and the throbbing at her temples increased its rapid beat.

She half staggered into the bathroom and frantically searched through a drawer for some Excedrin Extra Strength, quickly swallowing two tablets with a minimum of water scooped up in her hands. She hurriedly ran a washcloth under the faucet and stumbled back to the bed before applying it to her forehead. She shut her eyes and the noise and the throbbing grew worse. She could think of nothing except relief, and she lay there, gently sobbing in pain and misery, counting the searing pulsations at her temples as if she were counting sheep.

Relief did come mercifully fast and she must have dozed off, for the next thing she was conscious of was Oliver's coming into their bedroom and clicking on a light.

"Not feeling well?" he asked with what she thought was polite indifference as he stripped off the jacket of his jogging suit and headed for the bathroom. It took her a few moments to gain full consciousness and bring all the day's events into focus. She noted that her headache had, mercifully, subsided a bit.

Not rising from the bed, Emma called to him, "Did you have a good run?"

He came back out of the bathroom in his T shirt and underwear, holding his jogging suit and sneakers, heading for his closet.

"Yeah," he answered offhandedly

"It couldn't have been too vigorous," she said enigmatically.

"What?" he said, turning to face her on the bed.

"I mean," she said, "your shirt isn't even damp."

She could hear the sarcasm seeping into her voice, and she could see the muscles of his jaw twitching as he paused before answering.

"I stopped at Chanticleer's Tavern for a beer after my run," he said, trying to sound casual. "Ran into some people I know and we started talking."

Emma sat up on the bed. "Was Karen Phelps one of those people you just happened to run into?" She spat out these words like a hissing snake about to strike.

Oliver froze. Now his jaw muscles were twitching spasmodically and the silence in the room was thunderous. Both husband and wife seemed frozen in a *tableau vivant* that could have been titled The Moment of Truth. Then Oliver, resolving how he would play the scene, walked to the foot of the bed, still holding his jogging outfit and said, "Why do you ask that?"

Emma's headache, although much milder, had not gone away completely but now she was indifferent to it. She stared up at her husband.

"Because of this!" she said, fumbling in the pocket of her slacks and producing the now crumpled note which, in a burst of fury, she threw at him. He dropped his jogging suit on the bed and picked up the wadded piece of paper. She watched his face turn crimson as he unfolded the paper and recognized its content. Then he sat down at the edge of the bed with his back to her, and she instinctively drew her legs up, wrapping her arms around them in a protective crouch.

Still facing away from her, Oliver spoke. "Emma, I know how incriminating this must look," he said in a low, halting voice, "and maybe Karen and I have been too chummy lately, but I felt you were drifting away from me, from our family life together. Karen was very unhappy in her marriage, and one day I ran into her at Chanticleer's and we started to talk, and she opened up about her difficulties, and I was a convenient shoulder to cry on, and she was someone I could talk to about what was troubling me, and we just sort of drifted into this two-person support group."

All of this was said rapidly, with Oliver hardly taking a breath, and his voice grew lower as he reached the end.

"Have you slept with her?" she asked, her voice deadly calm.

Now he turned to face her. "No, Emma, I haven't!"

In the midst of her agitated state, with so many conflicting emotions rampaging across her brain, she looked into his eyes, saw the steady gaze, and heard the emphatic resonance of his statement and, somehow, she believed him. Now her anger took a sharp turn.

"So you didn't sleep with her but you just unburdened yourself by sharing with her all of my shortcomings as a wife and mother, is that it?"

His gaze never left her face. "Emma, Karen's a lawyer. She has a successful career outside of the home and I was hoping she could help me understand your recent need to find fulfillment outside our home, with your prison work.

He reached for her hand but she pulled back. Now he spoke in a tone that seemed to her to be like a bewildered little boy. "You can't say that things haven't been dramatically different around here since you got involved with the prison. I realized we were on the brink of a major rift that could destroy us as a couple, and I saw how adamant you were about not giving up your volunteer work, and I didn't want to lose you. I recognized that I had to change my thinking about this, and when Karen started talking about her troubled marriage, I thought she'd be someone who could help me see things differently—a professional woman's perspective."

Even in her angry and confused state, this all sounded so plausible, Emma had to admit, but her sense of betrayal in picturing Oliver telling Karen about their problems caused deep resentment, and she lashed out.

"You must have been a big help to her in solving her marriage problems, considering she's decided to leave her husband. Perhaps she was as helpful to you in making you see that your marriage was doomed, too."

Oliver rose from the bed and stood facing her. His voice intensified in pitch. "Karen's problems with Ken were entirely different from ours. Much broader. More fundamental."

"More fundamental than allowing me a sense of identity other than the glory of being your wife?" Emma shouted, matching Oliver's pitch, but adding sarcasm.

Oliver ignored her accusatory question. "Their marriage was beset with problems from the start, and I can't betray confidences and give you details."

Emma physically winced at this last statement and quickly retorted, "But you didn't feel you were betraying my confidence by sharing my defects with another woman?" She was conscious of light sobs escaping from her throat.

Oliver leaned across the bed toward her, and his eyes were blazing.

"God damn it, Emma, I was desperately trying to save our marriage—not looking for reasons to leave it!"

Then she saw his face crumple and swiftly change to the little-lost-boy look and his voice was cracking. "I'm sorry. I don't want to lose you. I'm trying to see your side," he wailed, struggling in his rising desperation. But she was not in a pitying mood.

"Well, now that Karen will be free shortly, maybe you'll rethink your situation and decide that divorce is the best course for you, too," she said, regretting the words even as they rushed forth from her mouth. "Then you can console each other without any pesky encumbrances," she added, as her eyes filled with tears, hating the sarcastic scold she had now become.

She wanted to escape this scene and all this turmoil and uncertainty, and she had a sudden urge to bury herself under the bed covers the way she did when she was a little girl and something bothered or frightened her. Instead, she returned his piteous stare with averted, wet eyes.

"That's a low blow, Emma, and you know it," was his last statement uttered in a wounded, defeated tone as he moved across the room to their bathroom.

She couldn't continue this confrontation any more; it was too painful and too destructive. All her conflicting emotions were jumbled together, causing her to strike out and not think clearly.

An unexpected thought flashed across her mind as she rose from the bed and dabbed at her eyes. She wouldn't think about this now; like Scarlet O'Hara, she'd think about it tomorrow. Her mother, the English professor, had always said that *Gone with the Wind* was very deserving of its Pulitzer Prize not just for the historical sweep of the novel but for the psychological complexities of its characters. Emma was now living a Scarlet moment and finding her responses similar to the fictional heroine's.

Emma did not want to be in the bedroom when Oliver returned. She crossed the room quickly and, standing in front of her dressing table, ran a brush through her hair and applied some lipstick in one sweeping motion, before going downstairs to join the kids in the family room.

43

The kitchen flowed into the family room. The dining room was used for Sunday dinner and formal occasions, but for everyday dinners the large, round table in the family room was used. Marta was busy setting the table, and Susie was perched on a stool in front of the breakfast bar, writing in a notebook. Emma greeted Marta and kissed Susie's temple.

"What are you and Daddy fighting about?" Susie asked in a solemn tone, not looking up from her notebook.

Emma was caught off-guard but quickly recovered.

"Oh, just the usual things married people argue about," Emma said smiling, hoping to sound casual.

"It sounded serious," Susie said, now raising her head and turning her gaze on her mother.

"Well, maybe it was a little more serious than usual," Emma admitted, "but nothing that we can't work out," she said, patting Susie's back and offering her another reassuring smile. She heard the words she was saying to her daughter and hoped she sounded convincing, because in her own troubled state of mind she wasn't sure that she and Oliver would work them out.

Not wishing to continue the discussion any further, Emma turned to Marta. "I'm starving! What's for dinner?" But she could feel her daughter continuing to stare at her. She knew tonight's dinner scene would be a long one in which she and Oliver would role-play the happy parents for the benefit of their kids, while the air around them crackled with hidden tension.

She heard a commotion in the front hall as Jonathan and Jeremy returned from walking the dogs and she was grateful for the distraction. The dogs came bounding into the family room, happily greeting everyone, and Emma found herself giving them a lot of frenetic attention, as Marta observed everything with a troubled frown.

44

On the surface everything went on as usual at the Granby home, but an underlying tension was evident to every household member. Contrary to her resolve to think about her marital issues *tomorrow*, Emma delayed focusing on the subject because her emotions were too raw and she didn't want to say or do anything that she would regret later. She needed time to calm down and think rationally.

Apparently Oliver was in the same holding pattern and acted like a caring husband and father without initiating any further discussion of how things stood between them. The children led their normal lives but they seemed unnaturally quiet in the presence of their parents, as if they were hoping to avoid causing, or witnessing, any flare-ups. Even Marta, a normally vivacious and cheery presence, went quietly about her work, frowning a lot.

Emma was acutely aware of the building tension among her family members but couldn't bring herself to directly address it. She wondered, and worried, if this current condition was driving Oliver more and more into Karen Phelps' arms. Was he sharing everything with her? Whenever she thought about his discussing her with Karen, her anger rose at the thought of what she considered a betrayal of family confidences, and she struggled not to build higher walls of resentment. Yet she had to admit that she also wished to share her current problems with some outside party that might offer an objective viewpoint. She wished her parents were still alive.

A week went by since finding the note, and Emma knew she had to take some action. Her imaginings of scenes between Karen and Oliver were becoming more elaborate, more intimate and more conspiratorial every day. She decided that she would violate her own sense of appropriateness and share her troubles with her friend and neighbor, Carol Mumford, the nearest thing she had to an intimate girlfriend.

"You want to take me to lunch?" Carol said, with great surprise when Emma called and extended a luncheon invitation, as this was not a common practice with the two friends.

"Yes," Emma said, aware of the urgency in her voice. "Let's go someplace where it's nice and quiet. I'd like to discuss something very important with you."

"The only place that fits that description is Laissez Faire over in Emerson. It's mostly a dinner crowd because people think it's too expensive for lunch."

Emma liked the idea of a meeting place in another town.

"Good, let's go there," she said quickly.

"Tomorrow?" Carol asked.

"No, I have my class at the prison tomorrow. How about Wednesday?"

"That's fine," Carol said, and then added, "Emma, I'm intrigued."

"I'll pick you up at noon," Emma said, not offering any information on what this lunch meeting was about.

The drive on Wednesday to Laissez Faire took over a half-hour, but except for the usual chitchat, Emma said nothing until they were seated in the sparsely populated restaurant at a rear corner table selected by Emma as affording the most privacy.

"I'm bursting with curiosity," Carol said emphatically after the waiter had brought them a bottle of wine and Emma told him they would order later.

Emma took a sip of wine and began her story. She was amazed to see how easily, how readily it poured out of her. Carol listened intently, never interrupting Emma's monologue. When Emma finished, she felt relieved, unburdened, but curious to get Carol's response

"Tell me the exact wording of the note that Karen Phelps sent to Oliver, if you remember it," Carol said, as her opening remark.

"I can tell you exactly," Emma quickly responded. "The words are seared in my memory." Emma then repeated the note, word for word.

Carol refilled her wine glass from the bottle of Chardonnay in the bucket at the side of the table before continuing. She noted the anxious look on Emma's face.

"I have to be honest with you, Emma," Carol said. "I've always thought your husband was a straight shooter. Women have an instinct about this. Now Karen Phelps is a notorious flirt and I had always heard through the gossip grapevine that her marriage was pretty shaky. And she's a damn good-looking woman, let's grant her that. But unless you and Oliver have been seething with mutual resentments for a long time and your bed has turned into an ice field, I can honestly say that I think it's entirely possible that he's telling the truth."

"No to the seething resentments and no to the ice field," Emma said, "except this last week." Both women smiled. "But

Oliver wants me to live exclusively for him and our kids, with no distracting outside interests. Is that reasonable? Is that fair?"

"Has he actually said that?" Carol asked.

"He said that my volunteer work at the prison is absorbing more and more of my time—not just my physical time but the time I spend thinking or worrying about my class, my students, my aide. He feels it's taking me away from him."

"You're a pretty intense person, Emma," Carol said benignly, "and you seem to have found a worthy cause to justify your intensity."

"But is it fair of him to resent my having found a cause I believe in? He's passionate about his work and I don't resent him for that."

"But his work has always been part of the deal. It's the engine that drives your comfortable life. Your volunteer work isn't bringing anything to the table that he's interested in, so he sees it as some new, unexpected pursuit that's taking you away from him."

"Carol, I'm not giving it up!" Emma said firmly, her face a fixed mask of determination.

"I don't think you should give it up. I just think you have to find a way to really talk things out and regain your sense of trust. I wouldn't let Karen Phelps ruin a marriage as solid as yours seems to be. Have you considered a marriage counselor?"

"No," Emma said quickly, inwardly shrinking from the idea of sharing her personal issues with a stranger.

"I know a very good one. I've used him myself."

"You?" Emma said, surprised.

"Sure!" Carol responded. "Gardner and I have had some rocky patches along the way—mostly my fault I guess—and the counselor we've used has been very helpful." Carol raised her wine glass. "Hell, we're still together, right? Give it some thought," she said, reaching across the table and patting Emma's hand.

The waiter approached their table and the two women fell into silence as they studied the menu. Emma, unburdened, now felt a surge of gratitude toward Carol who seemed eager to be supportive and to couch all of Emma's current issues in a positive, transitory light.

Whether it was the two glasses of wine she had consumed in the time they had been talking or the feeling of relief to have been able to finally share her problems with a sympathetic, generous friend, Emma was suddenly in a lighthearted mood and was more receptive to the idea of a marriage counselor, especially one that Carol recommended highly.

They both ordered a shrimp salad and spent the remainder of their lunch dwelling on lighter topics. Before leaving the restaurant Carol had written down the name and number of her marriage counselor and given it to a grateful Emma.

45

Upon returning home from her luncheon with Carol, Emma found a note from Oliver on her dressing table.

> *Emma,*
> *We can't go on like this. I'm sorry if you don't believe me when I say there was nothing between Karen and me except talk, and I know you feel betrayed even if that's all there was, but I tried to talk to you about the way I felt and you were very defensive and didn't seem to care. Now we don't seem to be able to communicate on any level and it's killing me because I love you and want us to be the way we always were before you started your work at the prison. I love you and want to work things out. I don't want to lose you, Emma. Please let's have a serious talk.*
> *Oliver*

Emma thought about Carol's description of Oliver as a straight shooter, and she felt that this note, with its underlying anguish, supported Carol's appraisal. Yet she also noted his reference to wanting things as they were before she started her prison assignment. Even if she believed him when it came to Karen

Phelps, her volunteer work was still the crux of their current problems. After dinner that night, over coffee, when the boys had gone down to the recreation room in the finished basement for ping pong and pool games and Susie had retreated to her room, still working on writing up her science project, Emma spoke.

"Oliver, I read your note, and I want to work things out, too," she said softly, with an encouraging smile.

Oliver's head shot up from where he had been studying his coffee, and he returned her smile, a clear look of relief and hope spreading across his face.

"I'm willing to accept your explanation about Karen, but that still leaves us with the problem of my work at the prison, which I'm not prepared to give up right now."

Oliver's smile dimmed, but Emma continued. "I really think we need professional help in working out this problem—a third party who can give us an objective view and help us reconcile our differences."

Emma paused, studying Oliver's expression to discern his reaction to her suggestion, but his face registered no response. She went on. "I have the name of a highly regarded marriage counselor and…"

"Highly regarded by whom?" Oliver interrupted her, but his voice indicated curiosity rather than challenge.

"By Carol Mumford," Emma said. "She and Gardner have used him for their own problems."

"And you discussed our problems with Carol?" Oliver asked, catching Emma off-guard.

"Yes, Oliver, I did. For the same reasons you discussed them with Karen Phelps: to try to get a better perspective on what was happening to us. You might be happy to know that Carol has a very high opinion of you, and she's very supportive of our working things out. That's why she shared with me that she and Gardner have used a marriage counselor and recommended him to us."

Emma studied Oliver's face. He seemed to be weighing this suggestion.

"Oliver, I truly believe that if we really want to address this problem of my work at the prison, we have to get an outside, professional view. I'm willing to do it. Are you?"

Oliver took a sip of his coffee and, placing the cup down with an air of resolution, looked directly at Emma, smiled and said, "Yes."

That night the temporary ice field that had formed in their bed melted under the heat of the make-up sex they enjoyed: warm, lingering and intense. The next morning Emma called the marriage counselor and made an appointment for Oliver and her to have their first session the following week.

46

That same morning Emma received a call from June Sperry, talking faster than usual in her eagerness to share the good news.

"Mercy's daughter, Hope, arrived yesterday to visit her mother. Oh, Emma, you should have seen how happy Mercy was!"

Emma smiled into the telephone, delighted to hear this news. Then she remembered Hope's long history with drugs.

"How is she?" Emma asked.

As if reading Emma's question behind the question, June responded with even more excitement.

"She's great! She's been off drugs for over a year, ever since leaving the rehabilitation center. She has a job and a boyfriend who, she says, has never taken drugs and keeps her on the straight and narrow. And she's become a born-again Christian."

June delivered all this information without taking a breath. After pausing briefly, she added, "She was planning to stay at a motel but I invited her to stay with me."

Emma marveled at how easily June had adopted Emma's concern for Mercy as her own, and with such generosity of spirit.

"Any news on the other daughter?" Emma asked.

"You mean Charity? No. But I really didn't ask," June said.

"I'd love to meet Hope," Emma said, knowing that any meeting would have to take place far from the prison.

"She's staying on 'til Sunday when she has to get back to her job in California," June said. "Why don't you come to my house for dinner?"

Emma thought quickly about June's suggestion and decided it would be like rubbing salt in a wound if she now extended the time she was spending on prison-related matters to missing dinners at home, especially at the current fragile state of negotiations with Oliver.

"I'm afraid I can't do that, but thank you. What time will you be home this afternoon?"

"Around four," June answered.

"Would you mind if I came by for a short visit at four-thirty?" Emma asked.

"Of course not," June replied, but her voice betrayed her confusion as to why Emma couldn't come for dinner.

"Good. Then I'll see you at four-thirty," Emma said, without offering any explanation for a short and precise visit.

That afternoon, Emma told Marta that she was running a few errands and would be back for dinner, as usual. Promptly at four-thirty, she pulled into the driveway of June's attractive colonial house. June's husband had been an executive with the local utility company but had died of a heart attach in his early forties, leaving June a young widow. Fortunately, her husband had several large insurance policies which left his widow in good financial shape if she lived conservatively. With a decent income, no mortgage and no children to focus on, June had poured her energies into her work at the prison hospital.

Although June's house was modest by Claremont Heights' standards, the exterior was well maintained and the landscaping was, now in late spring, lush and vibrant, reflecting, Emma thought, June's personality. As soon as Emma shut off her engine, she saw June standing in the doorway with a big smile and an irrepressible shake of her shoulders.

June greeted Emma like an old friend, with a big, spontaneous hug and ushered her into the cozy living room where Hope was sitting in a wing chair by the fireplace.

"Emma, this is Hope," June said with a friendly formality, and Hope rose from her chair and shyly held out her hand to Emma. In response, Emma surprised herself by ignoring Hope's extended hand and giving her a hug.

"I've heard a lot about you from your mother," Emma said, still holding Hope's shoulders and smiling. Emma felt a frail body frame beneath her fingers. Hope was only about five feet tall and fragilely thin. She had her mother's tan complexion and generous mouth, Emma thought, but her eyes, although large and wide apart like Mercy's, had a haunted look, so unlike Mercy's smiling eyes. Under Emma's scrutinizing gaze, Hope cast her eyes down and clearly looked uncomfortable.

Emma patted Hope's shoulder and released her. She took a seat next to June on a small sofa facing Hope, separated by a large coffee table filled with a tea pot, cheese and crackers, small sandwiches, cookies and fresh fruit. June urged Emma to take something to eat, but Emma, interested only in Hope and not wanting to be distracted in the short time she had for her visit, accepted only a cup of tea and, at June's insistence, a homemade cookie.

Hope was holding a plate with a half-eaten sandwich which June urged her to finish, but Hope seemed too anxious to focus on food.

"My mother talked about you a lot yesterday," Hope said, flashing a shy, half-smile in Emma's direction. "She really likes you."

"And I'm very fond of her," Emma said, returning the smile. "June is kind enough to keep me informed of how your mother is doing, and I know what it means to her to have you here now."

Hope looked away, and Emma could see tears at the corners of her eyes.

"My mother always tried her best and was there for my sister and me. It wasn't easy without a husband. My father was killed by a stray bullet in a gang shootout when I was five and Charity was seven. She raised us alone."

Now the tears were spilling down Hope's cheeks as she gazed off into the distance and continued speaking.

"I gave her so much heartache and trouble, but she never gave up on me. And as for Charity..." Hope paused and Emma saw her gulping air like some person fighting not to drown. "She broke my mother's heart...and after all my mother did for her...No one knows."

Hope hung her head and wiped her eyes with the sleeve of her blouse. June rose from the sofa and hurried to Hope's side, placing her arms around the downcast young woman. "There, there," June said, rubbing Hope's shoulders gently. "We understand."

Emma waited for Hope to regain her composure before saying anything.

"I'm sorry," Hope said, looking forlornly toward Emma. "But I can see how my mother's suffering and there's nothing I can do."

"The fact that you're here is all you can do for her now," Emma said, hoping to change the emotionally charged atmosphere.

"The only other thing that would bring Mercy great happiness would be to see your sister, too."

Emma was startled to see the total transformation in Hope's face. Her look of abject misery changed to one of angry resentment as her mouth grew stern and her eyes flashed with hard, piercing sparks.

"That's not going to happen," was all Hope said, in a voice filled with quiet intensity.

As strong an impression as Hope's look and sharp response had made on Emma, she would not give up.

"Perhaps if Charity knew your mother's condition," Emma suggested and was immediately cut off.

"She knows!" Hope said sharply.

"And she still refuses?" Emma asked with a clear note of disbelief.

Hope looked away again, and her face became a mask of bitterness and pain.

"She doesn't care!" She's got her nice little respectable life now with her nice home and her husband, the police officer, and her three kids, and she's forgotten about the past and doesn't want anything to do with me or her mother."

Hope's voice faltered and sobs interrupted her words. "I called her and told her. I begged her...I threatened her...but she's a stony-hearted bitch and she refused to come, or call or write."

Now Hope was gripped with hysteria. "She caused all this and she just wants to forget everything...to pretend it never happened...pretend she doesn't have a mother...or a sister either. If you only knew..."

Hope's words broke off in mid-sentence and she buried her face in her hands, her upper torso shaking with sobs, as June rubbed her back and tried to comfort her with soothing sounds.

Emma recalled the few facts she knew about Mercy's killing of Charity's boyfriend, and assumed that Charity had never found it in her heart to forgive her mother, even to the present day and under the direst circumstances. Emma found herself agreeing with Hope that Charity seemed very cold-hearted and relentlessly unforgiving, especially since her life in the ensuing years had evidently been happy and successful. Emma pondered the mysteries of the human heart, but then her mind hit on another idea.

"Do you think it might help if I called your sister?" she asked.

Hope raised her head from her hands and, looking directly at Emma through tear-streaked eyes, said, "It wouldn't do any good."

"But at least I could try," Emma responded quickly, betraying her own uncertainty and despair.

June had handed Hope several tissues, and the young woman wiped her eyes and cheeks and blew her nose before speaking.

"It's kind of you to try to help, but it won't do any good."

"At least let me try," Emma persisted, her own voice rising in emotional pitch as June and Hope stared at her. "We have nothing to lose by trying, right?"

"I guess not," Hope said with no conviction, but Emma felt a last vestige of hope rising inside her and impatiently wanted to act immediately.

47

"Do you have Charity's number handy?" Emma asked eagerly, rising from the sofa and approaching Hope. "Would she be home now?"

"She might be. She doesn't work," Hope said, reaching for her bag on the floor next to her chair and extracting a small, worn address book. June hurried to a nearby desk and returned with paper and pen. Hope read aloud a number and June copied it down.

"Why don't you use the phone in the den, and I'll stay here with Hope and we'll have some more tea," June suggested in her typically upbeat manner, pointing to a door at the far side of the living room. Emma started to walk toward the door, and then remembered something, stopped and turned.

"What's Charity's last name?" she asked.

"Wilson," Hope answered, still sniffling.

Emma heard June say "How about another sandwich," as she closed the door to the den and hurried to the phone on a small table next to a leather chair. She sat down and dialed the number from the piece of paper June had given her. After four rings, Emma was growing anxious when finally she heard a woman's voice say "Hello."

"Hello," Emma responded, assuming a cheery tone. "May I speak with Charity Wilson, please?"

There was a pause on the other end. "Who's calling?"

Emma heard the suspicious note in the unidentified voice and made an instant guess that the person at the other end of the line was Charity. Now she pondered how best to identify herself. Given Hope's description of how Charity refused to have anything to do with her mother, Emma thought the wiser approach was to mention Hope since, as strained as the sisters' relationship seemed to be, they were at least still occasionally speaking to each other. Acting mostly on impulse, Emma took a deep breath and forged ahead.

"My name is Emma Granby and I'm a friend of your sister's."

"What's wrong?" was the immediate response, asked in a cold, defensive tone. At least her assumption that she was speaking to Charity seemed to be correct.

"Nothing's wrong," Emma said quickly but then realized that she'd have to state her real reason for calling, and her words tumbled out with no clear strategy in mind. "Well, that is, I'm here with your sister and she's very upset because, as you know, your mother is seriously ill and nothing would give her greater pleasure than to see you…"

A quick, explosive interruption. "Did my mother ask you to call me?"

"No," Emma replied, trying to stay calm.

"Did my sister?" the question came like an angry jab.

"No, I assure you," Emma said, rattled by this attack mode. "I'm calling because if there was any chance that you could see your mother before it's too late, it would mean a great deal to her." Emma added, "And to Hope." Then Emma had a fresh idea. "If it's a matter of money, don't worry about that. I'll gladly pay your expenses.

"Just who the hell are you?" the angry voice now demanded.

Emma decided that she had to tell the truth. "I'm a volunteer at your mother's prison. I teach a class there and your mother has been my classroom assistant for the last two years. I consider her a good friend."

"Just what has she told you about me?" Charity asked, suspicion underlying each word.

Emma's mind was racing. "I know the horrible tragedy that happened."

"And what was that exactly?" Charity asked slowly in a lower voice now filled with hesitancy, Emma thought.

Emma reluctantly stated, "I know how your mother killed your boyfriend to prevent him from getting you hooked on drugs."

There was no response from Charity, and Emma hurried on. "I realize how awful that must have been for you, for everyone, but, Charity, your mother hasn't long to live. Couldn't you find it in your heart to forgive her? I beg you."

Charity's response was delivered in a voice quivering with emotion, bordering on hysterics.

"I can't visit her. I won't put my husband and children through that. I've put this all behind me. It's not a question of forgiveness. I just can't dredge up the past." A long pause and Emma thought Charity might have left the phone. Then, in a voice barely audible and choking with sobs, Charity spoke again. "Tell my mother that I'm sorry...that I love her...but I can't see her...and please don't call again." Now Emma heard an audible click and knew for sure that Charity had hung up.

48

Emma sat motionless, still holding the dead phone to her ear and struggling to make sense of what she had just heard. Charity was refusing to see her mother, even if it was her last chance, yet she was clearly very upset and expressing love for Mercy. And why was her concern for her husband and children outweighing her concern for her mother under such dire circumstances? Was the stigma of her mother in prison the only thing she thought about? Whatever her reasons, Emma concluded with a flash of anger, there seemed to be little charity in the daughter named for that virtue.

Finally she hung up the phone and returned to the living room where she found June and Hope sitting together on the sofa. Hope was listlessly eating a cookie at June's insistence. Both women looked expectantly at Emma when she entered the room.

Emma shook her head while extending her arms and then dropping them quickly to her side to express her sense of futility. "I couldn't persuade her. I'm sorry."

"Oh, dear," June exclaimed, raising a hand to her mouth, in an involuntary, childlike gesture to ward off unpleasant news. Hope just stared intently at Emma, as a pink flush rose on her face.

Trying to mitigate the pain of her announcement, Emma said, "She clearly loves her mother but she doesn't want to dredge up the past."

"I'll bet she doesn't!" Hope said sarcastically.

"She's very upset but she's also adamant, I'm afraid," Emma added.

"Well, at least Mercy has you, Hope," June said cheerfully, patting Hope's arm. Hope, looking glum, said nothing.

"We'll do the best we can for Mercy," June continued, but still there was no response from Hope who seemed lost in her own thoughts.

Glancing at her watch, Emma said, "I must get home for dinner. Hugging the silent Hope and the forlornly smiling June, Emma left June's home, feeling disappointed and confused by her phone call with Charity. On the drive home, she resolved not to allow her concern about Mercy to spill over into the evening's interactions with her family. Yet the very act of making this resolution angered and saddened her because she longed to be able to discuss the afternoon's events with Oliver, the way that he discussed difficult clients or challenging architectural details with her.

For all of their married life, and even before, they had been sounding boards and trusted advisors to each other on the minutia of their daily lives, until this prohibition on discussing her prison work had been imposed. It had been fine when Emma was discussing household issues or the children's problems or regaling him with local gossip, but the minute the borders of her life extended beyond what he considered permissible for her, he wanted to hear none of it. She had continued, as was expected, to listen attentively and react dutifully in offering feedback on his daily issues and concerns, but an important segment of her life had been placed off limits.

As Emma pulled into her driveway, she made a mental note to mention this unequal footing at their session with the marriage counselor.

49

The marriage counselor, a man named Eric Hutchins, was late forties, tall and thin, with sandy colored hair, pale eyes, a tentative smile and soft-spoken manner. Emma immediately felt comfortable with him, and Oliver wasn't showing any signs of uneasiness, although his answers to Eric's questions were much less expansive than Emma's.   But Emma reminded herself that Oliver was not a naturally talkative person.

In their first session, Eric had asked both Emma and Oliver to state in one succinct sentence what each perceived to be the current problem in their relationship.

Emma had volunteered first, saying, "I don't feel Oliver wants me to have any independent identity beyond that of wife, mother and homemaker."

Oliver, in turn, said, "My wife's volunteer work in the prison is taking her away from me and our kids."

When Eric asked Oliver in what way was the prison work taking Emma away from him and the kids, Oliver thought for a moment and then responded, "She's devoting more and more time and attention to the problems surrounding her students and especially her aide, Mercy."

Emma was quick to say, "My aide is dying of cancer and only one of her two daughters is offering her any comfort."

Eric then led Emma and Oliver in an exercise in which they individually wrote a list of all the things they liked about each other, that made their marriage good. Eric noted the ease and eagerness that both Emma and Oliver exhibited in completing a lengthy list of qualities they admired in their partner, only to find that they had listed many of the same qualities: sense of humor, intelligence, thoughtfulness, patience, well- grounded, good values, honest, loyal; romantic and passionate were also mentioned.

Only in the area of money did Emma and Oliver have markedly different attitudes. Oliver saw it as a visible indicator of his rise in the world from his impoverished childhood, while Emma, who had never known the discomfit of poverty, took it for granted. And when it came to social interactions, Oliver considered them important for his business but also enjoyable, while Emma mentioned that she often found their social gatherings superficial and boring, but she reluctantly participated in them from a sense of duty to her husband.

At the end of the first session, Eric said, "From what you've shared with me, it would seem that your marriage is a solid one in most aspects except for the current problem you've both identified."

Emma and Oliver shook their heads in agreement and Eric continued.

"It's obvious you both love each other and feel a deep commitment to your marriage and your family, so we have a firm basis on which to move forward and see if we can't reconcile your differences on this one area." Eric gave them a half-smile. "I'm confident we can."

Over the next several sessions—two a week—gently, supportively, Eric Hutchins guided Emma and Oliver in examining heretofore unstated attitudes that formed the basis for their current discontent. Emma's whole life prior to marrying Oliver had been spent in the shadow of her brilliant and vibrant parents. While she was cosseted and made to feel special, her role as an appreciative audience, content to bask in her parents' nimbus, was one she had accepted unflinchingly. They were the stars; she, a supporting player, a mere satellite in their dazzling circle. She had remained in their home and their orbit throughout her college years, only leaving its stunting security to marry Oliver and move into another subordinate role as helpmate to a talented, rising young architect. She drifted passively from one cocoon to another.

For his part, Oliver examined some underlying insecurities stemming from his own past. Unlike Emma's childhood of emotionally distant but doting and dazzling parents, who focused intermittently on their only child as an extension of their own superior gifts, when not focusing exclusively on themselves, Oliver's parents had been working-class, leading hardscrabble lives to take care of a brood of six children, and fighting continuously. Finally, Oliver's father had disappeared when Oliver was six.

Oliver had three older brothers who aspired to nothing more in life than a paycheck and a modicum of security, but he was the breakout kid, imbued with some mysterious gene that made him see the world with infinitely greater potential, and he resolved when still young to rise far above his parents and siblings.

From an early age, Oliver was constantly alert to possibilities, convinced that he possessed some talent that, if he could only discover it and then apply himself to refining it, would catapult

him into a higher economic and social niche than his family ever
dreamed of. A high school course in mechanical drawing was the
initial step in following a path that unlocked a talent which, when
combined with determination, perseverance, and a definite creative
flair, led him inevitably to a graduate degree in architecture from
Princeton, on a full scholarship, and a flourishing career.

In meeting Emma during his senior year at the university
where her parents were well-known stars and she seemed the
epitome of refinement and sophistication, he was immediately
smitten. Like a good merchant taking an accurate inventory,
Oliver was aware of his tall, strong body, his handsome, chiseled
face and a passion he felt for women that they seemed to
intuitively sense. He had been very successful during his
undergraduate years in attracting girlfriends, but his ambitious
goals always came first, and he had been content with short-term,
gratifying relationships until he met Emma. She became an icon in
his mind—a prize to win that would complement the position in
life he aspired to.

What amazed him about Emma was that despite her beauty
and brains and her self-indulgent inclinations, she seemed content
to subsume her future in his. He wouldn't consider marriage until
after he had finished his graduate work in architecture and had
established a first footing in his chosen profession, and she,
laconically, accepted these pre-marital terms with a passive
casualness that had delighted him and, until the recent past, had
been her behavioral pattern throughout their married life.

Oliver expressed his pride in having achieved his hard-earned
goals, even exceeding his financial dreams with his booming
architectural practice during the last decade, catering to the
wealthy inhabitants of Claremont Heights. His looks and manner

suggested a far higher pedigree than he could actually claim, and he admitted that he actively cultivated his rich clients not only for future business but also as a badge of acceptance. In this pursuit he regarded Emma, with her professorial parents, indulgent academic background—only the very secure majored in Latin and Greek in college—and casual, imperturbable poise, as a great asset. He took tremendous satisfaction in being able to provide a life of ease, security and even indulgence for his beautiful, loyal wife and his kids.

As he explored his feelings, under the gentle, coaxing guidance of the marriage counselor, Oliver came to understand that Emma's emerging need for an independent identity at this point in her life was threatening his well established and supremely satisfying self-image as being at the center of her life and the provider for all her needs—a living testament to all that he had achieved.

At one session, Emma had asked Oliver, "What about the time I tried being a real estate agent? You didn't seem to mind that."

Oliver smiled. "I thought that was just a passing fancy and wasn't I right? You quit after only a few months." His smile grew dim. "But this prison work is different. You're really invested in it."

In the course of their sessions, it became clear to Oliver that Eric Hutchins was trying to persuade him to understand and accept Emma's newly emerging need. Oliver, in observing the lifestyle of his wealthy and successful clients, acknowledged that many of the wives had interests outside of the home. Some pursued part-time careers as interior designers or real estate agents and a few were lawyers and even architects. In no case were the wives' pursuits for financial need but rather for personal fulfillment. They divided their interests between home and the outside world without doing any apparent damage to their domestic situation, except for perhaps a greater shifting of child-caring duties to their employed help.

In Oliver's case, he admitted, Marta filled that gap. The fact that Emma's outside pursuit was strictly on a voluntary, non-salaried basis, could continue to indulge Oliver's manly satisfaction derived from providing all her material needs.

Above all, what Emma (and Eric Hutchins) came to realize—to Emma's renewed delight—during these counseling sessions and the examination of feelings, was just how fiercely Oliver loved Emma and, in recognition of that ardent love, the compromises and adjustments he was willing to make to keep her happy. Gradually, Oliver came to see that merely tolerating her outside commitment was not enough; he had to accept it as an equally important aspect of her life, which she should feel free to share with him in strengthening their bond of mutual respect.

After much quiet reflection between sessions, Oliver conceded these points. For her part, Emma agreed that whenever any *major* conflict existed between her prison work and her family's needs, her family must come first.

Eric Hutchins led Emma to acknowledge that her children, despite their independent personalities, were still children. They needed their mother's guidance and emotional nurturance and should not be viewed as self-sufficient, in the same light that Emma's parents had regrettably, she admitted, viewed her.

Compromises on both sides were made in a recommitment of mutual understanding, acceptance and love.

50

"You've both made tremendous progress in our twelve sessions together," Eric Hutchins said, as he escorted the smiling couple to the door of his office. "If all marital problems were settled as quickly and as satisfactorily as yours, I'd be a much poorer man."

That night, in bed, after prolonged and ardent love-making, Emma gratefully shared with Oliver the details of what had recently transpired with Mercy, Hope, Charity and herself. From both Emma's tone and her descriptions, Oliver realized that the aide had touched a wellspring of compassion and concern in Emma that had not been revealed before.

Oliver listened attentively, his arms wrapped around her warm, soft body, her head resting against his chest and her words in feathery whispers gently blowing against his chest hairs. He wanted to show his support by suggesting more affirmative action, but he was stymied. All he could say, with an extra squeeze of her shoulders and a glancing kiss on her forehead, was "You must give Mercy all the support you can."

Emma kissed his neck, whispering "Thank you." Still cradling her, as though he held a soft, contented kitten, he could hear her slow, steady breathing before he, too, drifted off to a peaceful sleep.

51

Emma continued with her GED and writing class, but Mercy's absence only made her think of her aide more. After a week's stay, Hope had gone back to California but had promised to return. Chantelle, the fiercely proud African American, had left the class when her AIDS symptoms had grown worse. Chantelle's boyfriend, she discovered, had been sexually active with other women as well as men, and this bisexual behavior was known as acting "on the downlow." He contracted AIDS and passed it on to her. This news, coming on top of Mercy's death sentence and Stella's brutal beating, left the students morose and listless.

Nothing Emma did seemed to alleviate the general malaise pervading the group. Just when the class was at the low ebb, another shock hit the group. Anita, a pretty, young Latino woman, who had been convicted of drug trafficking but insisted that her boyfriend had, without her knowledge, hidden his stash in her apartment, was five months pregnant when she arrived at the prison, and, in due time, delivered a healthy baby boy.

According to prison regulations, Anita was allowed to keep her baby, whom she named Jesus, in the special nursery area where mothers were supervised and given training on how to take proper care of their babies. But the regulations permitted the babies to remain with their mothers for eighteen months, and at that time the babies had to be given to some relative on the outside or placed in foster care. Anita's boyfriend, the father of baby Jesus, was in prison, and Anita's only relative in the States was a sister who was a single Mom raising four children of her own, and she refused to take the baby. This meant that not only was Anita being separated from her baby, but it was being placed in foster care until she served the four years remaining on her six-to-eight year prison sentence or was paroled.

Since the majority of the inmates were mothers and suffering from the imposed separation from their children, Anita's sad case struck a responsive chord in their hearts, and an atmosphere of deep gloom descended on the class.

Despondent over losing her baby, Anita tried to commit suicide by cutting her wrists with a small piece of metal she had managed to get hold of. While her suicide attempt failed, the news only deepened the classroom gloom.

Emma encouraged her students to write about their feelings, and the sympathy and anger and maternal outrage poured out of them. The result of their expressing and sharing their feelings, however, was not a cathartic relief but rather an intensification of their strong sense of injustice and alienation.

Mariela, the class poet, shared a new poem she had written, called:

I See My Baby.
I see my baby smiling
But only in my dreams.
I hear my baby crying,
So real to me it seems.

I stretch my hand to touch him,
To feel his warm, soft cheek,
And touch his tiny fingers,
But in vain these things I seek.

No longer will he nestle
His head upon my breast,
And yawn and coo and yearn
To take a little rest.

I pray the Lord protect him
And keep him from all harm.
I see my baby resting
In someone else's arm.

I see my baby crying,
Surrounded by everything new,
But know, my dear, sweet baby,
Your mother's crying too.

Mariela read her poem in a maudlin tone that brought the rest
of the class, except for Helen, to tears or flashes of anger. Emma
felt she could not regain control of the class and lighten the mood,
so she cut the class short and, in a despairing mood, hastened to
Virginia Ryan's office. Now it was Emma's turn to cry, for as
soon as Virginia motioned her to take a seat and Emma started to
talk, the tears came.

"I can't take this, Virginia," Emma wailed. "It's
overwhelming me! Mercy's cancer and Anita's losing her baby
and attempting suicide and Chantelle's AIDS. My classroom is

one big cauldron of suffering and despondency, and I'm no longer able to teach. It's too much!"

Virginia listened with her usual attentive stare, and when Emma's voice trailed off, Virginia removed a box of tissues from her desk drawer and quietly handed it to Emma. The two women sat in silence while Emma dabbed at her eyes and wiped her nose. In a calmer voice, still trembling with emotion, Emma said, "I'm afraid I'm going to have to resign."

"That would be a shame," Virginia said softly, "because you're a damn good teacher."

Still sniffling, Emma said, "Maybe if I give up the teaching, I could be transferred to the medical unit. June Sperry tells me they're short on volunteers just now."

Virginia leaned forward across her desk and gave Emma a slight smile. "And then you could get to be with Mercy."

Emma looked down at her hands, playing with the used tissues, and couldn't return Virginia's frank stare. Then the streak of defiance, always so much a part of the spoiled child's and pampered woman's personality, was visible in Emma's eyes as she lifted her head and returned Virginia's stare. "I'm volunteering my services; I don't believe I have to supply a motivation."

Virginia laughed. "Emma, you're a pistol!" she exclaimed.

Emma remained silent.

"I know you've hit a rough patch, but I mean it when I say you're a damn good teacher." Virginia paused and looked away from Emma, as though she were weighing some decision. "I'll tell you what I'll do," she finally said. "Let's cancel your class for a few weeks and I'll bend the rules and arrange for you to see Mercy."

At the mention of seeing Mercy, Emma's eyes lit up, betraying her eager response to Virginia's words. "But only one visit, Emma," Virginia hastened to add. "That's all I think I can manage when I try to justify the visit by saying that Mercy was your aide. Any more than one visit would suggest some special bond, and I'd get a flat refusal from the administration."

A slow smile spread across Emma's face.

"Then we can see how you feel about continuing with the GED class. Does that sound reasonable?"

Afraid to speak and betray the full measure of excitement she was feeling at the prospect of being able to see Mercy, Emma simply nodded in agreement.

"Good!" Virginia said decisively. "I'll cancel your classes for the next two weeks—you're not feeling well, which is the truth— and I'll call you at home to let you know when you can visit Mercy."

Emma left Virginia's office suddenly feeling lighthearted and giddy, never having dreamt when she went flying to Virginia to unburden herself of all the morbid issues overwhelming her class that the result would be a near miracle: she was going to see Mercy again. This was happy news she could now share with Oliver. The thought of her new understanding with her husband added further joy to her gleeful mood.

PART FIVE

52

Each day Emma waited eagerly for Virginia's call, and when several days had gone by and she had heard nothing, she began to fear that Virginia had not been able to arrange for her visit to the prison medical unit to see Mercy. Emma realized that Virginia was bending the rules significantly. Five days after Emma's last visit with Virginia, the call finally came.

"Tomorrow afternoon at 2 PM," Virginia said in her usual crisp manner. "You can only stay for a short time, Emma, and this is definitely the only visit I could arrange without losing my job."

"I'm very grateful, Virginia," Emma said, her mind racing ahead to her visit with Mercy.

"Well, I just want to keep you as a teacher. I cancelled your classes for the next two weeks, so give me a call a week from this coming Friday and we can discuss your future, okay?"

Emma gladly agreed.

Exactly at 1:45 PM Emma passed through the huge iron-gated entrance to the prison with a warm smile for the dour guards and a heightened sense of excitement. Virginia had made all the arrangements and Emma was given a special pass to the medical unit, which was in another wing of the administration building. Passing quickly along different corridors and through two locked doors, she passed the ward for the mentally ill and finally arrived at the nurses' station for the physically ill.

Emma immediately looked for June Sperry but didn't see her. Directly behind the nurses' station was a small glass-enclosed room, harsh in the overhead florescent light, furnished only with one metal folding chair. Sitting on a stool reading a magazine, a guard was stationed at the door to the room. A sour looking nurse examined Emma's pass and then turned to the guard reading a magazine.

"Jeff, this lady is here to see Mercy Campbell," she said in a tired voice.

The guard, grossly overweight, lumbered off his stool and opened the door to the glass room. Expecting to visit Mercy in her hospital bed, Emma was momentarily confused.

"Have a seat and we'll bring her in, the nurse said to Emma, pointing to the metal folding chair, gleaming coldly under the florescent light. Emma stepped through the door, held open by the guard whose frown conveyed his annoyance at being interrupted in his reading. She sat on the folding chair and was instantly aware of being bathed in a brutally bright light, making her feel exposed and vulnerable, like a suspect under a spotlight, about to be aggressively questioned.

She was suddenly nervous and could feel perspiration at her temples as she shifted her weight, squirming in the hard metal chair. The light in the small glass room, which she judged to be no more than ten by ten feet, was so much brighter than the lighting outside the room that she could barely make out any figures at the nurses' station, contributing further to her sense of isolation.

Emma's stomach was churning and she felt an uncontrollable panic rising within her, when the door opened and Mercy, in a wheelchair, was wheeled into the room. Emma was flooded with relief and rose to greet her friend. She leaned over to hug Mercy, hoping that her shock at Mercy's appearance was not registering on her face.

In the two months since Emma had been separated from her aide, Mercy's deterioration was alarmingly evident. Mercy's body, always robustly compact, was, from what Emma could see beneath the white hospital gown and feel beneath her hands, boney to the point of emaciation. Her skin, always a glowing toffee colored sheen reflective of her Jamaican roots, now had a distinct sallow tinge under the bright light and hung in heavy creases across her cheeks and along her jaw. Mercy's eyes, always so sparkling with warmth and intelligence, were now lusterless beneath half-closed lids. A white bandana was wrapped sloppily around her head, with sparse clumps of hair peaking out at the hairline.

Mercy managed a half-smile, so different from her dazzlingly generous full smile that had bathed Emma in comfort and encouragement. The nurse who had wheeled Mercy in, left the room and closed the door and the guard took his seat on his stool, watching the room's two occupants.

"I'm so happy to see you, Mercy," Emma said with genuine enthusiasm.

Mercy took Emma's hands in hers and held them tightly.

"I've really missed you," Emma continued, and Mercy squeezed Emma's hands.

"I've missed you, too," Mercy said in a low voice, her words coming in a slow, faltering pattern. "How are the students?"

"Fine," Emma lied, making an instant decision not to add to Mercy's burden by telling her the sad news about Stella, Anita and

Chantelle, and the current gloom that had descended on the class. "Everyone misses you and can't wait for your return."

The corners of Mercy's mouth drooped. "I don't think that's likely," was all she said softly, gazing off into the distance.

Now it was Emma who squeezed Mercy's hands and said, "None of that talk," but she knew her words rang hollow and Mercy could see that her smile was forced. Emma pulled the metal chair closer to Mercy's wheelchair and took her seat again. The two women resumed their hand holding which seemed to give both of them comfort.

"I was so happy to meet Hope," Emma said, hoping to move the conversation to a lighter slant.

The corners of Mercy's mouth turned up sharply and she almost gave Emma a full smile, but the effort was too much for her and Emma saw the defeat in Mercy's eyes.

"Hope told me how nice you and June have been to her," Mercy said, her eyes suddenly moistening. "She's tryin' so hard to get her life together." Mercy paused and took a deep, labored breath before continuing. "She told me how you called Charity." Mercy's voice trailed off, and Emma knew they were back in deep, roiling waters.

"June opened her home to Hope and is the one who deserves all the credit," Emma said quickly, attempting to divert the conversation, but Mercy continued. "It was nice what you tried to do, but I understand why Charity doesn't want to open old wounds, and Hope should understand, too."

"Charity told me to tell you that she loves you," Emma said, trying to keep things on a positive note.

"I know she does," Mercy said quietly as tears wandered down the crevices of her cheeks. "I know she does."

"Is there anything I can do for you?" Emma asked, struggling to keep herself from crying. "Anything that you need?"

Mercy shook her head.

"You've been a blessing to me and I'm so glad to have the chance to see you one more time," Mercy said, and with these words, all pretensions were erased and the harsh, bright overhead light illuminating the two women seemed to pierce all pretense and reveal the stark reality that had been avoided to this point.

"But it's you who gave me so much help and guidance when I first came here. I could never have succeeded without you," Emma said, struggling to stay calm.

"You just had to find your own pace," Mercy said, giving Emma another half-smile, but she suddenly appeared very tired, and Emma realized that this meeting had taken great effort on Mercy's part.

The sour nurse rapped on the glass and pointed to her watch.

"It's time for more medicine," Mercy said apologetically.

Defying the rules, Emma leaned over and hugged Mercy, placing her head next to her aide's so that she could conceal the tears that were pooling in her eyes.

"Thank you for everything, Mercy," she whispered, knowing that this warm, generous woman had made her a better person. "It's been an honor to know you," she said softly, caressing Mercy's hollow cheek with her hand and thinking she could feel Mercy's life force at low ebb. "I'll keep sending messages through June," and there was a slight shake of Mercy's head. "And I'll stay in touch with Hope," she said as an afterthought.

The door opened and the nurse came briskly to the side of Mercy's wheelchair. "Time to go!" she said perfunctorily.

Emma looked into Mercy's half-closed eyes and smiled. She groped for the right thing to say. Her mind teemed with silly notions, like some frivolous hostess choosing good-night gestures to her guests, all of which seemed completely inappropriate since she knew that this was the last time she would see her friend. Then she decided that Mercy deserved more, and she could say nothing else at this final moment except the bare truth. She couldn't offer platitudes of false hopes about getting well or seeing you soon.

"I love you," she said simply and spontaneously, as a wave of emotion swept over her. Except to her parents, her husband and her children, she had never uttered the word *love* to another human being. This was Mercy's gift to her: the capacity to care about others, not just those intimately connected with her life; to look into the hearts of others and see the suffering, the good, the struggles; to find fulfillment in helping others less fortunate; to be constantly aware of manifold advantages bestowed on a person due to accidents of birth and the blessings of a positive, nurturing environment; to expand your humanity by embracing the humanity of others.

With what was obviously a great effort, Mercy looked directly into Emma's eyes, raised her hand and lightly touched Emma's cheek. "Thank you," was all she said, and now she seemed to be struggling to breathe.

The nurse was backing Mercy's wheelchair toward the open door. Emma quickly brushed the tears from her eyes and smiled as Mercy's crumpled body, looking like a child's in an oversized chair, disappeared from the arc of the room's harsh light. Emma stepped out of the glass room and stood still, watching the nurse wheel Mercy down the long aisle of the ward until all she saw was the white bandana on Mercy's head, glimmering against the dark gray walls, shading into black.

53

For the next two weeks, Emma stayed away from the prison, giving extra attention to her family but constantly preoccupied with Mercy's rapidly deteriorating condition.

"It's really only a matter of days, I think," June Sperry reported to Emma in her latest phone call, generously keeping Emma informed of developments. "I called Hope, but she's just started a new job and even if she could get the time off, she doesn't have the money for the air fare."

"Tell her I'll pay for the ticket," Emma said with no hesitation.

Emma told Oliver that night before dinner what she had offered to do. Oliver, true to his resolution to be supportive, immediately approved of Emma's offer. "The woman shouldn't die alone," he said with a conviction that reminded Emma of the younger Oliver when he wanted to design good houses for the poor.

The next day when Emma called June to confirm her offer of a plane ticket for Hope, June told Emma, "Mercy's sinking fast. Hope should hurry if she wants to see her mother before it's too late. I'll call her now." An hour later June called back to say that Hope could come on Friday—it was now Wednesday—and Emma called the airline, bought a round-trip ticket in Hope's name and arranged to have it delivered overnight.

Late, Friday morning, Emma met a haggard looking Hope at the local airport and drove her to the prison, dropping her off at the main gate before returning home.

Early Sunday morning, Emma received another call from June who sounded both tired and sad.

"It's all over, Emma," June said as soon as Emma answered the phone. "Mercy died peacefully this morning around 2 AM. Hope had stayed with her since Friday and on Saturday morning Mercy had recognized Hope and said a few words before sinking into a coma. Hope never left her bedside and never let go of her hand. It must have meant a great deal to Mercy to have Hope by her side. You made that happen."

Emma remained surprisingly calm upon hearing June's report, perhaps because her visit with Mercy just a few days earlier had confirmed in Emma's mind that time was very short and her leave-taking of Mercy had been done at that visit. With all Mercy's suffering, her death was now a blessing.

"Hope said her mother wanted to be cremated," June continued, "and Hope would like to take her ashes back with her. I'm making inquiries on the cost of it and if it's not too expensive, I'll pay for that."

Emma knew that June lived on a fixed income. She also knew that the prison authorities would put Mercy's body in a plain pine box and bury her in a barren, make-shift cemetery just outside the rear entrance to the prison, surrounded by a chain link fence, with tiny, crude wooden crosses denoting only the name of the deceased and dates of birth and death.

"Don't worry about the cost of cremation," Emma said with authority. "I'll take care of it."

"That's awfully kind of you Emma," June said, obviously relieved of a financial burden possibly beyond her means.

"How soon can it be done?" Emma asked, remembering that Hope was returning to California on Tuesday afternoon."

"The simplest process, without a casket and a wake can be done within a day of receipt of the body," June explained.

"Then let's do that, if it's okay with Hope," Emma said.

"Yes, I'm sure it would be," June responded.

June called back an hour later to report that everything had been arranged. Mercy's body would be delivered to the undertaker today and the ashes would be placed in a simple urn and delivered to June's house tomorrow afternoon.

"The cost is rather high, Emma," June said apologetically. "It's twelve hundred dollars. Please let me pay a part of it."

"Thank you, June, but no need," Emma said. "Give me the name and address of the undertaker and I'll run over with a check this afternoon."

Emma had instantly decided to draw money from her own account—money left to her by her parents—to pay this expense, although Hope's plane ticket had been paid for from the joint household account with Oliver's blessing. Emma's genuine commitment to Mercy made this decision very easy.

PART SIX

54

Tuesday afternoon was gray and drizzly, keeping with Emma's somber mood as she arrived at June's house and joined June and Hope in the living room. She immediately spotted the gray stone urn that was on a small side table next to where Hope, looking pale and tired, was sitting. Emma went to her and Hope rose and they embraced.

"I can't thank you enough for all you done for me and my mother," Hope said, her voice faltering with small, intermittent sobs.

Emma squeezed Hope's shoulders. "It was the least I could do for such a good friend as Mercy was to me."

"One of the last things she told me," Hope said, fighting back tears, "was to be sure to thank you and give you her love."

"I only wish I could have convinced your sister to visit and be reconciled with your mother," Emma said wistfully.

Hope sat down again and rummaged through her bag, extracting a pack of cigarettes and pulling one out of the pack. Then, with the cigarette dangling from her lips, she rummaged some more until she extracted a pack of matches from the bag and lit the cigarette. June had rushed out of the room and returned just as quickly with an ashtray.

Hope took a long drag on her cigarette and let the smoke out slowly through her nose.

"My mother was always reconciled with Charity," Hope said, delicately picking a tobacco sliver off her lips with her brightly polished nails.

"Then maybe a visit would have reconciled Charity with your mother," Emma said, recalling the killing of Charity's boyfriend.

Hope took another drag on her cigarette and looked off in the distance, away from where Emma and June were sitting opposite her on the sofa. There was an awkward silence as Emma watched Hope's face become a study in concentrated thought. Then Hope's eyes returned to the two women opposite her. She took another puff of her cigarette before nervously crushing it in the ashtray.

"I guess you deserve to know the truth," she said, exhaling the last bit of cigarette smoke. "Anyway, it doesn't matter any more. I kept my mother's secret while she was alive, and that's all I promised."

Emma leaned forward, tense with anticipation, as Hope brushed some cigarette ash off her slacks before continuing.

"My mother didn't kill Charity's boyfriend...and he wasn't really her boyfriend," Hope said with a slight, derisive laugh.

June let out a gasp of air and her hand flew to cover her mouth in that little-girl gesture that Emma had noted before. Emma sat stiffly, waiting for Hope to continue.

"The guy was my pusher, and he was trying to get Charity hooked on the stuff, just like I was."

Both Emma and June sat silently, transfixed by this revelation. Hope stared off into space and now spoke in a far-away voice as though she was reliving a traumatic scene in every indelible detail.

216

"My sister was a sweet kid, not at all like me. I was difficult and caused my mother a hell of a lot of trouble. She always forgave me and I knew she loved me no matter what. But my pusher—his name was Constantine—he was my boyfriend for a while before he turned me on to drugs. Then he dumped me once I was hooked. Constantine was real handsome and could turn on the charm. He started hangin' around and sweet-talkin' my sister and she fell for him.

"One day I came home and found him showin' my sister some crack and tellin' her 'Go on, baby, try it! You'll love it! I guarantee it.'

I went crazy and didn't want her gettin' fucked up...excuse me...messed up like me. So I ran into the kitchen and grabbed a big knife and threatened to kill him if he didn't leave her alone. He just laughed at me. I was hopin' just to scare him into leavin', so I made a move like I was goin' to stab him and then he grabbed my arm and was really hurtin' me and I dropped the knife.

"Now he was real pissed off and he punched me on the side of my head and I fell down and then he jumped on top of me and started slappin' me hard across the face, and he wouldn't stop. The blood was pourin' out of my mouth and my nose. Charity was screamin' because she thought he was goin' to kill me, so she picked up the knife and stabbed him in the back. He fell forward on top of me and didn't move.

"Charity started crying hysterically, and then I heard my mother's voice comin' from the doorway. 'Is he dead?' she asked. I turned my head and saw her standin' there with a bag of groceries in her arms. His face was lyin' against my shoulder and I could tell he wasn't breathin'.

'Charity, be still!' my mother said, and she put her groceries down and came toward me to pull Constantine's body off me. She checked his pulse. 'He's dead,' she said, and Charity started wailin' again. My mother took her by the shoulders and shook her hard. 'Stop that!' she hollered, and Charity stopped cryin' but was still sobbin'. 'Tell me quickly exactly what happened' she said. Charity told her everything. When she finished, my mother said, 'Charity, you sit down and get control of yourself. I have to think.'

"I got to my feet and saw a lot of blood on the front of my dress but didn't know if it was Constantine's or mine. My mother left the room and Charity and I stood still until she came back with a wash cloth and towel and washed the blood off my face. Then she handed me a plastic bag.

'Hope, go change your dress and put that one in this bag and bring it to me,' she said. She seemed real calm.

"I went into the bedroom that Charity and I shared—my mother slept on the couch in the livin' room. I saw my face in a mirror and it was all puffy and turnin' black around the eyes, and my mouth had a big cut on the side. I changed my dress quickly and brought the bloody dress back to my mother in the plastic bag. I saw her kneelin' over Constantine's body. He was lying face down with the knife still stickin' in his back. My mother was cleanin' the handle of the knife. Then she pulled it out of his back and—I couldn't believe my eyes—she was stabbing him in a different place.

"'What are you doin'?' I shouted. My mother stood up and faced both of us."

'Now listen to me,' she said, and she had a fierce look in her eyes I had never seen before. 'I'm goin' to call the police and when they get here I'm gonna tell them I stabbed Constantine, which will be true.'

"Charity started to wail again, but my mother shut her up with a wave of her hand. 'I'm gonna tell them that I came home and found Charity's boyfriend beatin' Hope and I couldn't stop him so I grabbed the knife and stabbed him. Hope, you can tell the true story of how you came home and found Constantine tryin' to get Charity to use crack and you tried to protect her by threatenin' him with the knife and then he turned on you and started beatin' you. You'll both tell it exactly as it happened *except* instead of Charity pickin' up the knife, I stabbed him. Is that clear?'

"I tried to say somethin', but my mother stopped me with another fierce look."

'Hope, you've messed up your life with drugs and bad companions and I hope this teaches you a lesson and you get your life back on track. Charity has always been a good kid and has ambition. I won't see her life thrown away by goin' to prison.'

"'But he could have killed me,' I cried."

'It's still manslaughter,' my mother said. 'Charity, remember: you were screamin' for Constantine to stop beatin' your sister when I came home, and I picked up the knife from the floor and stabbed him. Have you got that straight?'

"Charity was still whimperin' but she shook her head, yes."

Hope had been telling her story in a low, monotone voice as if she were seeing all the details right before her eyes. Now she paused and lit another cigarette, hungrily breathing in the smoke before continuing.

"The cops came and my mother took charge and told them the story like I just told you, with her takin' all the blame. The cops asked me and Charity some questions and we told them the same story. The cops talked to a few neighbors and they said they knew Constantine was a drug pusher and they had seen him hangin' around Charity. The neighbors said that Charity was a good kid but I was a lot of trouble to my mother, and I admitted to the cops that Constantine had turned me on to using crack. My bloody dress was handed over to them. They took me to the station and took pictures of my swollen face.

"My mother was handcuffed and taken away, and because she admitted killing Constantine, her trial was quick. Her public-defender lawyer tried to convince the jury that my mother was out of her head in tryin' to keep Constantine from killing her daughter, but the prosecutor argued it was still involuntary manslaughter and the crime called for a prison sentence. The jury agreed, I guess because my mother showed no sorrow for killin' Constantine. How the hell could she when she didn't kill him?"

Hope's voice rose to an anguished pitch with this last question, and she paused to take another puff on her cigarette. Emma noticed that Hope's hand was shaking.

"When the verdict was guilty and the judge gave my mother eight to ten years, Charity really broke down and started wailin', and I thought she was goin' to blab it all right there in the courtroom My mother was bein' led out of the courtroom and she turned to my sister and hollered 'Charity' in such an awful voice that half the people in the courtroom froze on the spot. Charity's head jerked up and she looked at our mother and we both knew by the look in her eyes that this was the way it was goin' to be."

Hope took another puff on her cigarette and looked up at the ceiling, speaking now in a softer voice.

"That was the last time Charity saw our mother. She met some guy on an army base about fifty miles from our town, and when he was shipped overseas they started writin' to each other. When he came back, he asked Charity to marry him and she accepted. They got married and moved to Chicago. He joined the police force and they had three kids, twin boys and a girl. No one ever knew what really happened except me and Charity and my mother...until now.

"I visited my mother in prison a few times and I felt miserable for her...for all of us...and I was takin' a lot of drugs and had a new boyfriend who was heavy into the stuff like I was, and he convinced me to take off with him for California. I agreed, and we lived on the streets and panhandled for food and drug money.

"We lived like that for over two years and I was afraid to write my mother the truth, so I made up stories about how well I was doin', but I always made some stupid excuse why she couldn't write me back. I'm sure she knew what was really goin' on. Then my boyfriend and I bought some bad shit and we overdosed and the cops found us unconscious in a park and rushed us to a hospital. My boyfriend died and I nearly did."

Silence fell on the cozy living room as Hope sucked on her cigarette again before extinguishing it in the ashtray.

"That was the turnin' point in my life. I told the hospital chaplain that I wanted to turn my life around, and he got me into a really good rehabilitation facility. I wrote my mother and confessed everything and she wrote back praisin' me for havin' the courage to make such an important decision and tellin' me she loved me and supported me.

"While I was in rehab, I called Charity and that's when I learned that her husband, Jack, knew nothin' about Constantine's murder or our mother bein' in prison. Charity has told Jack that her mother was dead. At first I was pissed that Charity wasn't supportin' our mother, but after a while I thought I understood why—Charity saw the chance to make a clean break and took it. I guess I don't blame her. It was a pretty awful story, and with her husband bein' a cop and all, I mean, I suppose I understand, but I don't feel close to her as a sister should.

"I would have stopped callin' her if my mother didn't ask for news about her and the kids, so I'd call Charity once in a while and pass along news about the kids and how well the family was doin', and my mother loved that and never asked why Charity never contacted her directly. She seemed to know why and understood. Then, after she died and I was goin' through her things, I found this."

Hope halted and started searching in her bag until she produced a snapshot and handed it across the coffee table to Emma who examined it: a picture of a pretty, light skinned African-American woman, looking to be in her early thirties, sitting on a park bench surrounded by three smiling children, two boys identical in appearance, both about six, and a little girl, even lighter toned than her mother, about four, self-consciously posing in a frilly dress. Their eyes were squinting in the bright sunlight but, still, Emma could see the sparkle and warmth of their grandmother's eyes.

Written on the snapshot, Emma read, "All my love, Charity, Scott, Thomas and Ava."

55

Emma passed the picture to June as Hope said, "Charity must have sent that picture to our mother in the last few months cause the boys are only about six now."

Emma smiled at Hope but her thoughts were no longer on the picture. She was thinking back to Mercy's favorite saying, "Things aren't always what they seem." Now Emma understood that Mercy's understanding and sympathy for others, her inherent dignity and kindness, stemmed from the guarded secret of her own family and her willingness to sacrifice her own life for her daughter's security and happiness.

The nagging doubts that, on some subconscious level, Emma had always harbored, unable to reconcile Mercy's gentle, caring nature with the one horrible act of violence, were finally vanquished. Emma now exultantly told herself how right she had been in assessing Mercy's true character and how justified in embracing Mercy as a loving friend. Then she thought of Mariela, who admitted taking a human life but suffered endless agonies of remorse and was truly, endlessly contrite for her one, violent act. Wasn't she worthy of being befriended, too, Emma reasoned, given the model prisoner she had become in the ensuing long years in prison?

Emma's thoughts were interrupted by June's exclamation, "Of course, she loved her mother deeply!" Emma turned to see June's bright eyes filling with tears. She patted June's arm before turning her attention back to Hope.

"Thank you for sharing this with us," Emma said. "I can't tell you how much it means to me."

"You deserve to know the truth," Hope responded. "seein' how kind you were to my mother. She was a real special person."

"Yes, she was," Emma said, rising from the sofa. "And her special qualities, and the heroic sacrifice she made, will be our living memory of her that only the three of us and Charity will share."

June added, "Yes," and Hope, smiling, rose from her chair and picked up the urn with her mother's ashes.

"I'd like to keep this for a while," Hope said solemnly. "It makes me feel close to her, after all the years that we were separated."

Emma smiled and nodded, but Hope continued, "If you have any idea what you think might be a good place to scatter them eventually, I'd love to hear from you."

Emma sensed that this request was really a veiled plea to keep in touch, and she decided immediately that she, too, wanted to keep in touch with this fragile young woman to honor Mercy and perhaps act in her stead.

"I'll give it a lot of thought, Hope," Emma quickly replied, "and I promise I'll be in touch with you soon. I've got your address and phone number and you have mine. Don't hesitate to call."

"My goodness, look at the time," exclaimed June, pointing to her watch. "I've got to get Hope to the airport or she'll miss her plane."

The three women walked together through the modest kitchen and out the side door to the driveway where June's car was parked. Emma could see Hope's battered suitcase already in the back seat. June got behind the wheel while Hope stood by the passenger door. Emma drew Hope quickly toward her. In this close embrace, Emma could feel the urn that Hope was still holding pressing against her heart, and she was acutely aware of Mercy's abiding presence.

PART SEVEN

56

The following morning, as Emma was having her second cup of coffee, she received another call from June Sperry with one of her breathless deliveries. "Emma, have you heard?" June asked, her voice rippling with excitement.

"Heard what?" Emma said, slightly annoyed.

"Virginia Ryan was attacked yesterday at the prison. She was stabbed by an inmate who had the delusion that Virginia was keeping her from getting paroled."

"Stabbed?" Emma said, trying to wrap her mind around this news.

"Yes," June said hastily, "with a ball-point pen that the inmate had stolen from the superintendent's office when she was cleaning it. She made the point sharper by grinding it against the cement wall of her cell. It's not a serious wound. The woman was aiming for the heart but it only pierced Virginia's breast."

Emma felt as though she could breathe again. "It's a blessing Virginia is amply endowed," she said, almost in a joking manner, strictly from relief. "How is she?"

"She's at Canfield Hospital for I don't know how long," June said. "I'm going to visit her this afternoon and I thought maybe you'd like to go with me."

As fond as she had grown of June, Emma resisted her invitation. June would be full of concern and solicitude for Virginia, and Emma felt that Virginia would not want or appreciate that. She wanted to see Virginia, of course, but not in June's company.

"I can't make it this afternoon, June," Emma said, without giving any explanation. "You go ahead and I'll see her this evening."

June offered no protest and their conversation ended after a few brief pleasantries. Now, as Emma returned to her coffee and sat solemnly alone in the breakfast nook, her family having gone off for the day, she had time to digest this latest event and once again her thoughts floated back to Mercy.

During the half-hour or so that they had spent together before class every Tuesday and Thursday, and Emma, curious about a living environment so different from anything she had ever known, would tentatively ask questions about prison life. Mercy would answer, first with brief responses and, later, when their friendship and mutual trust blossomed, with fuller, often disturbing descriptions.

"You put nearly a thousand women behind bars, in cramped little cells, like wild cats in a sack," Mercy had explained, "and you've got all sorts of personalities respondin' to a total loss of freedom, with the guards constantly tellin' them what to do, and the whole place is just full of tension. You live day to day, never knowin' when some woman is going to crack or when you might crack because you can't stand it any more. You're always lookin' around, watchin' everyone for signs of anger or frustration that's about to explode, and you pray it's not comin' in your direction. It's like you're in a war and going out to fight every day but never knowin' where the enemy is comin' from. It's probably the worst part of life in prison, except for separation from your loved ones, because you never think of it until you're here and you're livin' it. This place is like a pot with a steady, simmerin' flame under it that could boil over at any second."

Emma thought of the inmates in her class, who all had to have good conduct records to qualify for the GED program, and even within this small group, how their spirits flowed and ebbed, and how in their writing they suggested the extraordinary pressures they faced in trying to stay sane and focused in such a hostile environment. Even the insights she gleaned from their writing, she knew, were only glimpses of the true hellish dimensions of prison life. Then she thought it was a wonder that there weren't many more women becoming delusional and going berserk, and how it must have felt for Mercy to know that she had entered this sordid and violent world voluntarily and was saving Charity from all these horrors.

Emma wondered if she could do the same for Susie, but dismissed the thought quickly without arriving at any conclusion, for fear that she would find herself lacking in such a heroic spirit. Yet this brief rumination led to increased admiration for the quality of Mercy's sacrifice.

Even as a volunteer, Emma had entered a prison, so alien to every aspect of her experience, to find a prisoner who had expanded her appreciation for life beyond anything she had learned from her professorial parents, her first-rate education or her sophisticated, successful friends. The person she was now, after her two years with Mercy, was, she reflected, remarkably different from the person she had been.

Emma knew that, like the urn with Mercy's ashes that brushed against her heart when she had embraced Hope, Mercy would forever be a presence in her life. Blinders had been ripped from her eyes, and she viewed the world with a much wider vision of how anyone's place in society was mostly an accident of birth. Nobility and courage and dignity could be found in any human soul, regardless of background or education or class. You only had to be receptive to discover it, with no biases, no limitations.

Finishing her coffee, Emma dialed the local florist to order flowers to be sent to Virginia Ryan. Then, on a sudden impulse, she called a national service and ordered a floral arrangement to be sent to Hope in California, with the message. "Thinking of you and your wonderful mother. Love, Emma."

57

When Emma arrived at Canfield Hospital that evening, she found two other volunteers and Virginia's secretary in Virginia's room. Virginia was sitting up in her hospital bed, a woolen shawl drawn around her shoulders against the cool air-conditioned temperature of the room. Emma gave Virginia a quick, awkward hug.

"I got your flowers," Virginia said, seeming in good spirits and pointing to a large bouquet next to several others. "They're lovely. Thank you. My family was here earlier and they were amazed at all the bouquets."

"This place looks like a tropical garden," Mary Calahan, Virginia's secretary, said, waving her hand toward the profusion of flowers arranged about the room. Everyone smiled politely. "Most of the arrangements look like they came from a florist, but mine came from my garden," Mary said with a hint of pride. The two other volunteers, whom Emma did not know, started talking about their gardens, and the chatter flowed easily. Both Emma and Virginia listened with attentive looks but said little.

From somewhere in the corridor a bell rang and Virginia explained that visiting hours were ending. The awkward hugging ritual was repeated, and as all four visitors were leaving the room, Virginia said, "Emma, could you stay for a minute longer?"

The other ladies paused and, sensing that Virginia wanted a private exchange with Emma, smiled and exited gracefully. Emma returned to Virginia's bedside and, following Virginia's invitation, took a seat nearest to the bed. Virginia chuckled. "That's really the fifteen-minute warning bell, but I wanted a chance to speak to you alone."

"How long will they keep you here?" Emma asked, and Virginia, waving her hand dismissively, said, "Just another day or so."

"What a horrible experience for you!" Emma said, reflecting her true feelings. "I was shocked when June Sperry told me."

Virginia flicked her hand dismissively again. "It comes with the territory. The woman who stabbed me said she heard voices telling her that I was responsible for blocking her parole each time she was eligible for it. The voices also told her she had to get rid of me if she ever wanted to get paroled. Poor thing! Now she'll serve her full time and several years more, in the psychiatric ward."

Virginia paused and gave Emma one of her searching stares. "You've been through a lot yourself. I'm sorry about Mercy. How are you doing?"

Emma had not expected the conversation to shift so abruptly to her, and she flashed a smile and looked away, trying to collect her thoughts. Rather than answer Virginia fully, she said, "Okay. Will you be returning to your job when you're better?"

"Yes, sure!" Virginia said matter-of-factly and then added, "How about you, Emma. Do you want to continue volunteering at the prison?"

Emma looked down at her lap. "I don't know." Then she looked up at Virginia and there was uncertainty and confusion in her voice as all her conflicting thoughts tumbled out. "You've just been stabbed by a prison inmate who, in a delusional state, fixated on you, and yet you say without hesitation that you want to return to that same environment that's so rife with violence. You don't seem phased at all by what's happened to you, but I have to admit, it scares the hell out of me. I don't know if I want to be in an environment that can't offer me security...where I'll constantly feel anxious and at risk. It took a while for my husband to reconcile himself to my working in the prison and I haven't told him about your being stabbed. If he found out, I know he would insist that I stop volunteering immediately for the sake of our children as well as for me and him. I can't honestly say that I would blame him or that I could, in good conscience, go against his wishes."

Emma could feel herself coming close to tears, and she stopped talking abruptly and looked down at her lap again. A momentary silence ensued before Virginia spoke.

"You paint a pretty grim picture, I must admit. And your husband would have every right to insist on your quitting if he knew what we know about prison life."

Virginia reached out and, cupping Emma's chin in her hand, gently raised Emma's head to meet her gaze. This gesture, so uncharacteristic of Virginia's crisp, professional style, took Emma totally by surprise. Virginia released her grip now that she had Emma's full attention.

"I'll tell you a secret, Emma. I don't just look upon my work as a job. I look upon it as a vocation. A special calling, if you will. When I was a kid, I thought a lot about becoming a nun, surrounded as I was with all the nuns in my Catholic elementary and high schools. Then as I got older and found myself irresistibly attracted to certain boys and thinking a lot about getting married and having a family, yet I still thought about being a nun and I was very conflicted. When I fell in love and married Tom, my husband, and our kids started arriving, I was happy in the choice I had made, but a small amount of conflict never left me, for I admired the nuns' self-sacrifice and dedication to others and considered it, if not a higher calling, certainly a very noble one. Yes, I was dedicated to my husband and my children, but that was from a very satisfying personal love, and didn't seem comparable to an ability to dedicate yourself to caring for others whom you didn't love but who needed you—a going out of yourself, so to speak—and finding a spiritual connection with others much different from yourself, who did not necessarily appreciate anything you did for them. I thought of this kind of service as a special vocation. My husband, who had been in a junior seminary as a teenager and joined the Peace Corps after college, understood my feelings and has always supported me in my work. In college, I thought of nursing and teaching as *giving* professions, but I didn't feel suitable for either. Then in the summer of my junior year, I read an article in the local paper about a young woman sent to prison on drug charges who had been brutally attacked by a fellow inmate and, in despair, had committed suicide, and I instantly knew I wanted to work in prisons."

Virginia paused and adjusted her shawl more tightly around her shoulders. "I don't know why they keep it so cold in here," she said irritably, before returning to her confidential tone. "I've never regretted my decision, Emma. As Tom took on engineering jobs in different places and the family relocated with him, I worked in four different women's prisons before landing here. Each situation was unique, and all were challenging, but I knew that I had achieved the best of both possible worlds: fulfillment as a wife and mother and in my special calling to try to help women whose lives are so dramatically different from mine and who are branded for life and discarded by society as being worthless, shunned by nice, respectable people, and condemned to lead lives of quiet desperation.

Pausing again to adjust her bed covers, Virginia smiled at Emma.

"So that's the context in which I choose to view this latest incident. For over twenty years I've been on a journey exploring my special vocation and have been blessed to work in a field that kept challenging me as a professional and kept me growing as a person. Now I've hit a little speed bump, but that only spurs me to renew my efforts and continue my special work. Am I making any sense?"

"Yes," Emma said, returning Virginia's smile. "I can see why you consider this special work and I can certainly say that it's made me see the world in an entirely different light."

Before Emma could say anything further, Virginia interrupted her. "I'll tell you another secret, Emma. A lot of volunteers come through my office, and I never question what motivates them to volunteer in a prison, although I suspect for a lot of them it's prompted by a feeling of *noblesse oblige* or a thrill-seeking desire to vicariously experience the outer fringes of society. For others it might be to gain the spotlight at chic dinner parties with outrageous stories of prison happenings and having people marvel at their spunk for venturing into this unknown, dangerous world. My suspicions are usually confirmed by the short duration of their stay, or when they come face to face with reality as opposed to their imaginings. But then there are the others—the special ones—

the volunteers who show real potential for seeing their work in a different light. June Sperry was one of them. And you're another. It's nothing definable; just some capacity to look within yourself and recognize a kinship, a human connection with the inmates that gradually seduces you into a firm commitment. Hell, it's like missionary work, only instead of going to a foreign country to help the poor and ignorant, you're descending into the bowels of your own society to help the outcasts."

Emma was surprised and pleased to hear Virginia's designation of her as a special one. Indeed, when she thought of Mercy and all her students, she was quick to admit that they had taught her much more than she had taught them, and she also admitted that, given the circumstances most of them had to endure, she could have become an inmate too. Yes, she certainly felt a kinship with most of them on a broad human level, and, yes, she wanted to help them in any way she could. Still, the burden of involvement, of caring, was a major one, and she honestly didn't know if she could sustain it and also give unstintingly of herself to Oliver and the children.

Virginia studied Emma's pensive look and said. "Do you know what Mariela, your class poet, told me about you?" Emma shook her head. "She said, 'I always knew I had a body, but Mrs. Granby showed me I had a mind.' That's your special gift, Emma."

On hearing these words, Emma felt very proud that she had evoked such a profound testament from her brightest student.

"You've got another week before you're due back to class," Virginia said, interrupting Emma's thoughts. "I hope to be back to work by then, so think it over and give me a call."

The intimacy of exchanging their deeply personal thoughts and feelings so frankly made Emma want to tell Virginia about Mercy's not killing her daughter's boyfriend but taking the blame to protect her daughter. She started to speak but then checked herself, feeling she shouldn't violate Hope's confidences. Instead, she said, "Thank you for all you've shared with me, and for all your help and support. You've given me a lot to think about."

Just then, a nurse appeared at the door of Virginia's room and said, "Sorry, time to go."

"Give me a hug," Virginia said, extending her arms toward Emma with a broad smile, "but gently because I'm still sore."

Emma gladly leaned delicately into the circle of Virginia's arms and Virginia whispered, "Remember, you're one of the special ones."

PART EIGHT

58

The ballroom of the largest downtown hotel was crowded for the annual awards luncheon sponsored by the administration of the nearby women's prison. The prison superintendent, along with various staff members and local dignitaries were duly applauding as Virginia Ryan called the names of volunteers to come up and accept a plaque for various lengths of service, beginning with one year and moving on to multiple years.

After honoring four volunteers for five years of service, Virginia Ryan said, "If you've volunteered for five years, we know you're hooked and we don't want to spoil you, so we skip to ten."

Virginia waited for the small ripple of laughter to subside before continuing. "Today we have one volunteer to reach that milestone. I did a little research yesterday and discovered that this person is responsible for over one hundred women earning their high school equivalency certificates. Please join me in thanking a special volunteer, Mrs. Emma Granby, for ten years of dedicated service."

June Sperry, sitting next to Emma and scheduled to receive a twenty-year award next year, patted Emma's hand and Emma rose and walked to the podium where Virginia was waiting, holding a plaque.

"It gives me great personal pleasure to award you this plaque," Virginia said, smiling directly at Emma, "and on behalf of the administration, to thank you for your outstanding work."

Emma quickly glanced at the plaque that Virginia handed her and then turned to face the audience as Virginia stepped back from the podium. Emma's heart was beating wildly as she listened to the sustained applause. When it stopped, she spoke directly into the microphone perched atop the podium.

"Thank you, Mrs. Ryan and Superintendent Skelly. I could never have achieved this milestone without the support and encouragement of my husband, Oliver, and the understanding and cooperation of my three children, Jonathan, Jeremy and Susie, all of whom are here today." Emma looked directly at her beaming family. "I love you and thank you." Then she shifted her body slightly in the direction of Virginia. "You, Mrs. Ryan, have been a continuous tower of strength and inspiration who helped me through challenging days and who is the very heart of the entire corps of volunteers. My very special thanks to you."

Emma paused and took a deep breath before continuing. "Finally I must acknowledge the one person who, more than anyone else, is responsible for my receiving this ten-year award. Her name is Mercy Campbell and she was my first educational assistant when I began teaching the GED program. It was she who encouraged me to bring patience and humor and flexibility to my classroom, and she who taught me not to accept things as they appear and not to judge, and she who guided me in developing a compassionate and empathetic spirit. Although she died eight years ago while still in prison, her presence has never left me and is with me now. Mercy, I thank you for making me a better teacher and, by your example, a better, fuller and richer person. Thank you all very much."

Emma looked out across the clapping audience to the dark recesses of the ballroom where she could visualize Mercy: her huge dark eyes, the gleaming toffee-colored skin and that broad smile with the dazzling white teeth. They had come a long way, together. Emma smiled, not so much at the audience but at her dear friend.

AFTERWORD

While this is a work of fiction and the setting is a nonspecific Midwestern prison, the bones of the story are based on real-life observations by a very good friend who spent many years working as a volunteer in several women's prisons—recall the staggering statistics of over two million Americans behind bars in 2009, one-fourth of the entire world's prison population and disproportionately comprised of minorities.

It was my friend who witnessed so much injustice under the banner of law and order, and the dehumanizing effects of prison life. It was she who recounted the harsh and often brutal backgrounds that spawned lives inevitably leading to the prison gates. And it was she who pointed out the unforgiving nature of a society that offers so little in the way of rehabilitation or assistance to women prisoners during and after their incarcerated years. Branded for life as "ex-cons," and therefore denied job opportunities and the second chance of a clean slate, the women return to the environments that fostered their clashes with the law, thereby condemning them to most likely repeat their mistakes.

In recounting real-life stories to me over the years, my friend aroused my conscience and inspired me to write this book that, while fictional, still aspires to depict a segment of society that is little understood, mostly shunned and seldom offered any compassion. We administer punishment but deny redemption.

Invisible behind bars, safely locked away from our consciousness and consideration, they inhabit an alternate world we seldom glimpse and little comprehend.

May this book light one candle of hope and concern.

Richard V. Barry